U0165784

超實用

銀行英語單字

Practical Banking English Vocabulary

楊曜檜 著

書泉出版社 印行

INTRODUCTION
作者序

　　本書以介紹銀行、郵局等金融機構實務工作經驗常碰到的常用英文單字為主。特別針對三大對象加以設計編寫：

　　一、在銀行、郵局、信用合作社、農會、漁會等金融機構上班的行員。因工作所需必須掌握實務中常用到的金融英語專業辭彙，故本書適用作為各大金控、銀行、郵局的員工教育訓練的基本教材。

　　二、本書適合作為專科、大學商學院等相關科系課程的正規教科書或參考書。眾所皆知，不少大專院校的商學院的教科書都用原文書來授課，不少學生光是為了理解原文書中的財金英文單字意義就花了不少時間在查字典。本書除了收納銀行行員實務中常用的金融英文單字外，也收錄了不金融、國貿、財金用語，將實務與理論完美地融合為一體。

　　三、出國旅遊或留學民眾。在國外旅遊或觀光，常需到當地的銀行辦理兌換外幣或是兌現旅支等外匯業務；而留學生更是常需跟國外當地的銀行往來，如辦理開戶或是換匯等。但

金融英語是屬較專業英語，一般人也不知道如何用日常生活的英文來表達金融專業辭彙，因此如能掌握本書所介紹的金融英文單字，到了國外也不用擔心如何和當地銀行打交道。

　　本書在編寫上，力求正確詳盡，除了筆者在金融機構的實務工作經驗外，筆者費時三、四年走遍數十家本國銀以及外商銀並搜集、整理實務上常用到的銀行英文關鍵用語以嘉惠金融行業人員和有心學習金融英文的學子。筆者在編寫此書過程中，發現不少坊間金融英文相關的書籍介紹的英文並非老外的標準講法。例如不少書聲稱「定存中途解約」的英文是說 release the time deposit before maturity 來表示，但實際上老外表達「解約」時，完全不會考慮 release 這個動詞，而是用 cancel 或 terminate。筆者在編撰此書中，遇到疑難的英文表達用語，都一定向筆者所熟識的美籍副教授請教，以道地老美的觀點來協助筆者翻譯正確的英文，以力求本書的道地性和正確性。此外，筆者也請多位不同銀行的行員對此書提供意見和校對，以達盡善盡美。

　　最後，因各金控、銀行等金融機構的相關法令、規定或相關活動經常變更、修改，故若本書介紹的各銀行以及產品內容如與各銀行、郵局、農會、漁會、信用合作社等金融機構的

公開揭露資訊有不一致之處，請以各銀行、金融機構的公佈資料為依據。本書雖經多次編輯校對，但仍恐有疏失之處，尚祈各界前輩先進不吝指正。

NOTE 筆記頁

NOTE 筆記頁

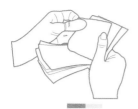

一般交易篇

GENERAL TRANSACTION

GENERAL TRANSACTION
一般交易

▶ 中文	▶ 英文
(ATM的)明細表；收據	(n.) receipt
(中文字)以正楷書寫；(英文字母)以印刷體書寫	(v.) print
(公司戶的)大章	(n.) stamp
(公司用來收發的)印章；蓋章於…	(n.) (v.) stamp
(公司發給行員的)名片	(n.) business card
(存款)餘額；平衡	(n.) balance
(存款機的)存款口；出鈔口	(n.) deposit slot
(行員別在胸前顯示姓名的)名牌	(n.) name badge = name tag
(定存)中途解約處罰	early withdrawal penalty

GENERAL TRANSACTION
一般交易

▸ 中文	▸ 英文
(定存)期滿;到期;存期	(n.) maturity
(定存、保單等的)解約;取消	(n.) cancellation
(定存、保單等的)解約;取消	(v.) cancel
(定存;支票;保單)到期	(v.) mature
(定存;保單)展期;續約	(n.) renewal
(定存;保險)展期;續存;展期	(v.) renew
(定存到期)解約並轉入活存兌現;(基金)贖回	(v.) redeem
(金額數字的)大寫	(n.) word
(金額數字的)小寫	(n.) figure
(保全用的)甩棍	(n.) baton

GENERAL TRANSACTION
一般交易

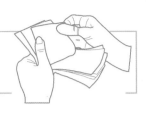

▸中文	▸英文
(英文)大寫字母；資金	(n.) capital
(原留簽名的)印鑑	(n.) specimen signature
(匯款的)收款人姓名	(n.) beneficiary name
(匯款單上的)備註；附言	(n.) sender-to-receiver information
(銀行)帳戶；戶頭	(n.) account
(銀行)擠兌	(n.) bank run = run on the bank
(銀行營業辦理交易的)截止時間	(n.) cut-off time
VIP快速櫃(通常為VIP使用)	(n.) express counter
一次付清；一次付清的款項	(n.) lump sum
一致的；符合的	(adj.) consistent

GENERAL TRANSACTION
一般交易

▶ 中文	▶ 英文
人手不足的；人力短缺的	(adj.) understaffed
人頭戶	(n.) dummy account
入帳；信用	(v.) (n.) credit
下屬；部下；部屬	(n.) subordinate = inferior
大額存款	(n.) large deposit = large-lots savings
子帳戶	(n.) sub-account
小冊子；DM	(n.) brochure
不一致的	(adj.) inconsistent
不計息帳戶	(n.) non-interest account
不寄發對帳單的帳戶	(n.) non-statement account
中止；(定存、保單的)解約	(v.) terminate

GENERAL TRANSACTION
一般交易

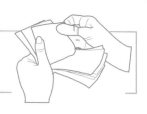

▸ 中文	▸ 英文
中途解(約)	(phr.) terminate ... before maturity = terminate ... before the maturity date = cancel ... before maturity = cancel ... before the maturity date
中途解約	(n.) early termination = early redemption
允許透支保障功能	(n.) overdraft protection = bounce protection
公司戶	(n.) corporate account
公司章	(n.) company chop
公用事業費	(n.) public utility bills
分行	(n.) branch bank = bank branch
分行引導員;白手套	(n.) branch ambassador = usher = lobby leader

GENERAL TRANSACTION
一般交易

▶ 中文	▶ 英文
分部	(n.) division = department
切結	(n.) undertaking
午餐券	(n.) luncheon voucher
反詐騙；反詐騙的	(n.) (adj.) anti-fraud
反詐騙專線	(n.) anti-fraud hotline
戶口名簿	(n.) household certificate
戶名	(n.) account holder's name
戶籍地址	(n.) registered address = permanent address
戶籍謄本	(n.) household certificate transcript
手機號碼	(n.) cell phone number

GENERAL TRANSACTION
一般交易

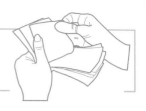

▶ 中文	▶ 英文
手續費	(n.) bank fee = bank charge = service fee = service charge = handling charge = handling fee = commission charge = commission fee
手續費;索取費用	(n.) (v.) charge
支存;甲存	(n.) current deposit
支存戶(支票存款帳戶);甲存戶	(n.) checking account = current account
支存戶;甲存戶	(n.) current account (英式英語)
文件	(n.) document
主要的	(adj.) primary
主要帳戶	(n.) principal account

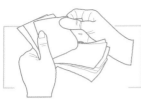

GENERAL TRANSACTION
一般交易

▸ 中文	▸ 英文
主要證件；第一證件	(n.) primary identification
主管；上司	(n.) supervisor = superior
代收付	(n.) agency collection and deduction
代收付業務	(n.) commission collection and payment
代理人帳戶	(n.) nominee account
代辦業務	(n.) agency service
出生日期	(n.) date of birth
出生證明書	(n.) birth certificate
可動用餘額	(n.) available balance
可轉讓定存單	(n.) negotiable certificate of deposit (NCD)
外國人；外國人的	(n.) (adj.) alien
外幣戶	(n.) FOREX (FX) account = foreign currency account

GENERAL TRANSACTION
一般交易

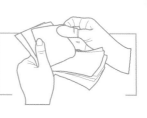

▸ 中文	▸ 英文
本人親自	(phr.) in person
本金	(n.) principal
本金自動展期	(n.) automatic principal renewal
本國銀行	(n.) domestic bank
未成年人	(n.) minor
民營化	(n.) privatization = going private
永久居留證	(n.) Alien Permanent Resident Certificate (APRC)
甲、乙種活期性存款	(n.) demand deposit = sight deposit
申請	(n.) application
申請人姓名	(n.) the name of applicant = customer name
申請書	(n.) application form = form
企金	(n.) corporate banking

GENERAL TRANSACTION
一般交易

▸ 中文	▸ 英文
企金客戶；公司戶	(n.) corporate customer
企業員工銀行服務	(n.) employee banking
全功能櫃臺	(n.) full service counter
印泥	(n.) ink paste = seal paste
印章	(n.) seal = Chinese seal = personal seal = name chop
蓋印章	(v.) seal
印臺	(n.) ink pad
印鑑卡	(n.) specimen signature card
同事	(n.) coworker
同意書；契約	(n.) agreement
名字	(n.) first name = given name

GENERAL TRANSACTION
一般交易

▸中文	▸英文
回沖(到信用卡帳戶)	(n.) chargeback
多變的	(adj.) variable
存戶	(n.) depositor
存本取息	renewal and interest drawing = principal-receiving and interest withdrawing time deposit
存期；存款期	(n.) deposit tenor (常以複數形出現)
存款；定金；存(款)	(n.) (v.) deposit
存款；儲金；儲蓄	(n.) savings
存款收據；存根聯	(n.) deposit receipt = paying-in stub
存款信封	(n.) deposit envelope
存款保障	(n.) deposit protection

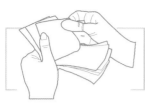

013

GENERAL TRANSACTION
一般交易

▶ 中文	▶ 英文
存款條；存款單	(n.) deposit slip = deposit form = deposit request form = deposit ticket = paying-in slip
存款證明	(n.) deposit certificate
存摺	(n.) passbook = bankbook / bank bank = deposit book = account book
年收入	(n.) annual salary
年利率	(n.) annual percentage rate (APR)
成年人	(n.) adult
收款人	(n.) remittee = beneficiary = payee
收款銀行	(n.) beneficiary bank
有效的護照	(n.) valid passport
死亡證明書	(n.) death certificate

GENERAL TRANSACTION
一般交易

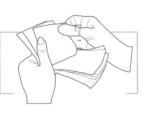

▶ 中文	▶ 英文
自動展期	(n.) automatic renewal
行銷DM	(n.) sales literature
佣金；手續費	(n.) commission
低利率的	(adj.) low-interest
免除(手續費)	(v.) waive
免填單據的服務	(n.) slip-free service
利差	(n.) interest rate spread
利息	(n.) interest
利息收益	(n.) interest return
利息所得	(n.) interest-earning
利率	(n.) interest rate
呈交；交…	(v.) submit = tender
投資銀行	(n.) investment bank = merchant bank
更正	(n.) rectification

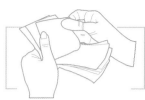

GENERAL TRANSACTION
一般交易

▶ 中文	▶ 英文
每日最高轉出限額	daily maximum transfer out limit
每月總收入	(n.) gross monthly income
每年	(adv.) per annum = every year
沒收	(v.) confiscate
沒有使用銀行服務的	(adj.) unbanked
私人銀行業務	(n.) private banking
身分證	(n.) personal identification card = personal ID card
身分證件	(n.) identification (ID)
身分證字號	(n.) ID number
使…作廢；無效的	(v.) (adj.) void = make something void
到期支票	(n.) matured check
到期日	(n.) maturity date = due date

GENERAL TRANSACTION
一般交易

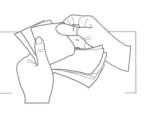

▸ 中文	▸ 英文
協理；副總經理	(n.) senior vice president
取(款)；提(錢)	(v.) withdraw = draw (口語) = take out (口語)
取款；提錢	(n.) withdrawal
受託人；被授權人	(n.) agent
固定利率	(n.) fixed rate
固定利率定存	(n.) fixed rate time deposit
委任；委派	(v.) delegate
委託人；授權人	(n.) principal = grantor (of the power) = donor (of the power)
委託書	(n.) letter of proxy = mandate = power of attorney (POA)
姓	(n.) surname = last name

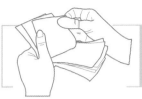

GENERAL TRANSACTION
一般交易

▸ 中文	▸ 英文
定存	(n.) fixed deposit = term deposit = time deposit
定存存單	(n.) time certificate of deposit = term certificate of deposit = fixed certificate of deposit
定存單	(n.) certificate of deposit (CD)
定存質借	(n.) time deposit pledge
定期儲蓄存款	(n.) time savings deposit
居民	(n.) resident
居留證	(n.) Alien Resident Certificate (ARC)
性別	(n.) sex
拒絕往來戶	(n.) dishonored account
服務臺	(n.) information counter

GENERAL TRANSACTION
一般交易

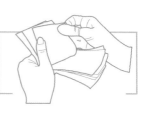

▶ 中文	▶ 英文
法定代理人	(n.) statutory representative
直接扣繳；自動扣款	(n.) direct debit
空殼公司	(n.) dummy company
表格；單據	(n.) form
金庫	(n.) vault = the strong room (英式英語) = coffers
金額	(n.) amount
信用合作社	(n.) credit cooperative associations
信用報告	(n.) credit report
信託戶	(n.) trust account = account in trust
便宜的；合理的	(adj.) reasonable
便服日	(n.) dress-down day

GENERAL TRANSACTION
一般交易

▸中文	▸英文
保全	(n.) security guard = security
保管帳戶；託管帳戶	(n.) custodian account
保證金交易	(n.) margin trading
宣傳手冊	(n.) pamphlet
客戶	(n.) client = clientele (總稱)
客戶群	(n.) customer base
指定扣款帳戶	(n.) designated payment account = designated debit account
政治獻金專戶	(n.) dedicated account of political donations = campaign contribution account

GENERAL TRANSACTION
一般交易

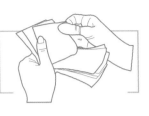

▶ 中文	▶ 英文
活期儲蓄帳戶	(n.) demand savings account = passbook savings account
相片	(n.) picture
紀念鈔	(n.) commemorative banknote
紀念幣	(n.) commemorative coin
約定帳號	(n.) designated account number = specified account number
美鈔；一元美鈔	(n.) greenback = buck (俚語)
衍生管制帳戶	(n.) derivative watch-listed account
負餘額	(n.) debit balance
借方；扣除	(n.) (v.) debit
個人退休帳戶	(n.) individual retirement account (IRS)

GENERAL TRANSACTION
一般交易

▸ 中文	▸ 英文
凍結帳戶	(n.) blocked account = frozen account
原留印章	(n.) original chop
原留印鑑樣式	(n.) original specimen seal
員編	(n.) employee number
核對簽名	(n.) signature verification
消金	(n.) consumer banking
消費券	(n.) consumption voucher
海外帳戶	(n.) offshore account
祕密戶；保密戶	(n.) confidential account
討論會	(n.) forum
財務長	(n.) Chief Financial Officer (CFO)
起息日	(n.) value date
逆差	(n.) adverse balance

GENERAL TRANSACTION
一般交易

▸ 中文	▸ 英文
偽幣	(n.) counterfeit coin = bogus coin = spurious coin = forged coin = phony coin
假鈔	(n.) counterfeit note = bogus note = false note = spurious note = forged bill = phony bill
健保卡	(n.) Health IC card
副本；第二聯；副本的	(n.) (adj.) duplicate
副理	(n.) assistant manager = sub manager
副總；協理	(n.) vice president
商業銀行	(n.) commercial bank
國外匯款	(n.) foreign remittance
國外銀行	(n.) overseas bank

GENERAL TRANSACTION
一般交易

▸ 中文	▸ 英文
國定假日	(n.) bank holiday
國際提款；國外提款	(n.) international withdrawal
國籍	(n.) nationality
執行長	(n.) Chief Executive Officer (CEO)
婚姻狀況	(n.) marital status
專戶	(n.) dedicated account
將(錢)存入(戶頭)	(phr.) deposit into = put into = pay into
帳戶餘額	(n.) account balance
帳號	(n.) account number
帳管費	(n.) account management fee = account service fee = account maintenance fee = maintenance fee

GENERAL TRANSACTION
一般交易

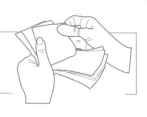

▶ 中文	▶ 英文
得來速銀行；汽車銀行	(n.) drive-through banking = drive-thru banking = drive-in banking = car banking
接待處	(n.) reception desk
掛失	(n.) loss reporting
掛號信	(n.) registered mail
授權；放行	(n.) authorization
教育程度	(n.) education attainment
現金取款	(n.) cash withdrawal
現鈔箱	(n.) cash drawer
第二的	(adj.) secondary
第二證件	(n.) secondary identification
通訊地址	(n.) correspondence address = mailing address
通提	(n.) interbank withdrawal

GENERAL TRANSACTION
一般交易

▸中文	▸英文
通儲	(n.) interbank deposit
透支	(v.) overdraw
透支；透支額度	(n.) overdraft
透支帳戶	(n.) overdraft account
透支額度	(n.) overdraft line = overdraft amount
最低餘額	(n.) minimum balance
單利	(n.) simple interest
單據 ；(存 、取、匯款)條	(n.) slip
提款條；取款單	(n.) withdrawal slip = withdrawal form = withdrawal ticket = withdrawal request form
無摺戶	(n.) paperless account = savings account without a passbook = non-physical account

GENERAL TRANSACTION
一般交易

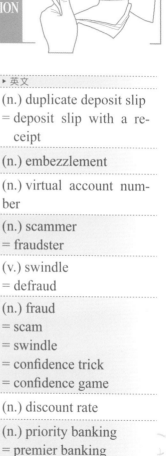

▸ 中文	▸ 英文
無摺存款單；兩聯式存款單	(n.) duplicate deposit slip = deposit slip with a receipt
盜用公款	(n.) embezzlement
虛擬帳號	(n.) virtual account number
詐欺犯；詐騙集團團員	(n.) scammer = fraudster
詐騙	(v.) swindle = defraud
詐騙；詐騙案	(n.) fraud = scam = swindle = confidence trick = confidence game
貼現率	(n.) discount rate
貴賓理財；優先理財；尊榮理財	(n.) priority banking = premier banking = privilege banking
週休二日	(n.) five-day workweek

GENERAL TRANSACTION
一般交易

▸ 中文	▸ 英文
郵局	(n.) post office
郵政儲金	(n.) postal savings
郵遞區號	(n.) zip code
鈔票；紙鈔	(n.) banknote = note = bill
開戶	account opening
開戶行	(n.) account opening bank
集保戶	(n.) safekeeping account
順差	(n.) favorable balance
黃金存摺	(n.) gold passbook = gold bankbook
黃金投資	(n.) gold investment
黃金基金	(n.) gold fund
黃金帳戶	(n.) gold account
傳真號碼	(n.) fax hotline = fax number
傳票；憑證	(n.) voucher

GENERAL TRANSACTION
一般交易

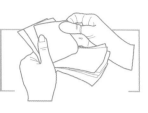

▶ 中文	▶ 英文
匯出行	(n.) remitting bank
匯票；郵政匯票	(n.) money order (M/O) = postal order
匯款；寄錢；過戶；匯款	(v.) (n.) transfer = remit = send = wire
匯款；匯款單	(n.) remittance = transfer
匯款人	(n.) remitter = remittor
匯款手續費	(n.) remittance charge
匯款通知	(n.) remittance advice
匯款單；匯款條	(n.) remittance slip = remittance = remittance form = remittance request form = remittance bill
塗改；變造；竄改	(v.) alter

GENERAL TRANSACTION
一般交易

▸ 中文	▸ 英文
填上日期；寫上日期	(v.) date
填寫(申請書)	(phr.) fill out = fill in
暗記	(n.) anti-counterfeiting mark
會議	(n.) conference
會議	(n.) meeting
會議室	(n.) meeting room
照會；查詢	(n.) inquiry = enquiry (英式英文)
經理	(n.) manager
經辦	(n.) person-in-charge
董事	(n.) director
董事長	(n.) chairman of the board
解付行；匯入行	(n.) paying bank
跨行匯款	(n.) interbank funds transfer

GENERAL TRANSACTION
一般交易

▸ 中文	▸ 英文
運鈔車	(n.) armored cash-transport car = armored car
運鈔箱	(n.) cash in-transit box = CIT box
電子存單	(n.) electronic certificate of deposit = online certificate of deposit
電子金融轉帳	(n.) electronic funds transfer (EFT)
電話號碼	(n.) telephone number
零用錢	(n.) pocket money
零存整付	fixed deposit by installments = odd deposit and lump drawing
零錢；換(錢)	(n.) (v.) change (不可數名詞) = small change = loose change

GENERAL TRANSACTION
一般交易

▸ 中文	▸ 英文
預約週期轉帳	(n.) scheduled recurring transfer
預約轉帳	(n.) scheduled funds transfer = pre-arranged funds transfer
對保;擔保;保證	(v.) certify
監督;失察	(n.) oversight
監督;監理	(v.) oversee = supervise
監護人帳戶	(n.) custodial account
綜合存款帳戶;綜存戶	(n.) omnibus account = integrated account = composite deposit account = all-in-one account = deposit combined account
蓋(章);簽上(簽名)	(v.) affix

GENERAL TRANSACTION
一般交易

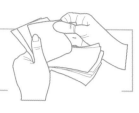

▶ 中文	▶ 英文
認識您的客戶	(phr.) know your customer (KYC)
銀行	(n.) bank
銀行名稱	(n.) bank name
銀行存款證明	(n.) certificate of bank balance
銀行行員	(n.) bank worker
銀行家；銀行業者	(n.) banker
銀行業務；銀行業	(n.) banking
銀行職員	(n.) bank clerk
銅板；硬幣	(n.) coin (有可數和不可數用法)
餌鈔	(n.) bait money
廣告傳單；宣傳單	(n.) flyer
影子銀行	(n.) shadow banking

GENERAL TRANSACTION
一般交易

▶ 中文	▶ 英文
撲滿	(n.) piggy bank
樣本	(n.) specimen
潛在客戶;潛力客戶	(n.) potential client
確認;核對	(n.) verification
稽核(人員)	(n.) auditor
稽核	(v.) (n.) audit
複利	(n.) compound interest = compounding
餘額查詢	(n.) balance check = balance inquiry = balance enquiry
駕照	(n.) driver's license
整存零付	lump-sum saving for small withdrawal
整存整付	lump-sum deposit and withdrawal = lump deposit and drawing

GENERAL TRANSACTION
一般交易

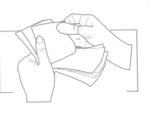

▸ 中文	▸ 英文
整批轉帳	(n.) batch remittance
機動利率	(n.) floating rate = flexible rate = variable rate
機動利率定存	(n.) variable-rate time deposit
融資帳戶；保證金帳戶	(n.) margin account
辦公室的隔間	(n.) cubicle
辦公室戀情	(n.) office romance
靜止戶；久未往來戶	(n.) inactive account = dormant account = inoperative account = unclaimed account
優惠存款	(n.) preferential interest deposit
儲蓄帳戶	(n.) savings account
營利事業登記證	(n.) business license
營業時間	(n.) banking hours = business hours

GENERAL TRANSACTION
一般交易

▶ 中文	▶ 英文
營業執照或登記證號碼	(n.) Registered Certificate Number
總行	(n.) headquarters (一定要加s) = head office
總經理	(n.) president
聯行戶	(n.) inter-branch account
聯行匯款	(n.) intra-bank funds transfer = Inter-branch funds transfer
聯絡人	(n.) person to contact (PTC)
薪資戶	(n.) payroll account
襄理	(n.) junior manager
殭屍銀行	(n.) zombie bank
櫃臺；高櫃	(n.) counter
櫃臺行員；櫃員	(n.) teller
禮券	(n.) gift voucher

GENERAL TRANSACTION
一般交易

▶中文	▶英文
覆核;核對;驗(章/簽名)	(v.) verify
額外費用;附加費用	(n.) surcharge
簽名	(n.) signature
簽名	(v.) sign
繳納營業稅證明	(n.) business tax payment certificate
證券戶	(n.) securities account
證券交易帳戶	(n.) brokerage account
證券存摺	(n.) securities passbook
證明書;證照	(n.) certificate
關戶;銷戶	(phr.) account closing
關懷;關心	(n.) concern
警示帳戶	(n.) watch-listed account
續存	(n.) deposit renewal
護送	(v.) escort

GENERAL TRANSACTION
一般交易

▸ 中文	▸ 英文
護照號碼	(n.) passport number
顧客	(n.) customer
顧客滿意度	(n.) customer satisfaction (CS)
顧客滿意度調查	(n.) customer satisfaction survey
權力；權限；權威；權柄	(n.) authority
贖回；兌換	(n.) redemption
鑑定；識別	(v.) identify

NOTE 筆記頁

自動化銀行業務篇

AUTOMATED BANKING

AUTOMATED BANKING
自動化銀行業務

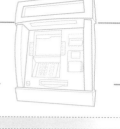

▸ 中文	▸ 英文
(ATM的)按鍵	(n.) keypad
(正式的)通知；告知；通報	(v.) notify = inform = apprise
(金融卡、存摺等的)補發	(n.) replacement
(網銀的)交易密碼；理財密碼	(n.) transaction password
ATM循環機	(n.) cash recycling ATM
Google的手機作業系統平臺	(n.) Android
分配；吐(鈔)	(v.) dispense
叫修	(n.) service call
企業網路銀行	(n.) business online banking = B2B (business-to-business)

AUTOMATED BANKING
自動化銀行業務

▸ 中文	▸ 英文
吃(卡)	(v.) swallow = eat = retain = keep
存摺密碼	(n.) passbook password
扣款	(v.) debit
自動化銀行服務；無人銀行服務	(n.) automated banking services = automated services
自動叫號機	(n.) automatic queuing machine
自動存款機	(n.) Automated Deposit Machine (ADM)
自動存款機	(n.) Cash Deposit Machine (CDM)
自動扣繳	(n.) automatic bill payments
自動提款卡；金融卡	(n.) ATM card

Automated Banking
自動化銀行業務

▸中文	▸英文
自動提款機	(n.) Automated Teller Machine (ATM) = automated cash dispenser (英式英語) = automated cashier = automated banking machine (ABM) = bank machine = cash machine = cashpoint = money machine = Money Access Center (MAC) machine
行動銀行	(n.) mobile banking = mobile phone banking
位數；數字	(n.) digit
更新；補(摺)	(v.) update
取代；補發	(v.) replace
取回(卡片、現金、收據等)	(v.) retrieve

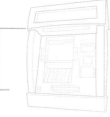

AUTOMATED BANKING
自動化銀行業務

▸ 中文	▸ 英文
取號機	(n.) number machine = ticket dispenser
服務	(n.) service
直效銀行	(n.) direct banking
金融卡	(n.) bank card
保養;維護	(n.) maintenance
計算;算計	(v.) calculate
計算機	(n.) calculator
重新上磁	(v.) remagnetize
重置成本	(n.) replacement cost
個人網路銀行	(n.) personal online banking
時間鎖	(n.) time lock
消磁	(v.) demagnetize
動態密碼	(n.) One-Time Password (OTP) = dynamic password

Automated Banking
自動化銀行業務

▶ 中文	▶ 英文
動態密碼產生器；密碼小精靈	(n.) OTP token
國外提款功能	(n.) international with-drawal functionality
密碼	(n.) password = Personal Identification Number (PIN) = secret code = PIN code = PIN number
密碼函	(n.) password envelope
密碼輸入器	(n.) code input keyboard
帳戶明細	(n.) itemized account data
帳戶明細	(n.) itemized account re-cords
帳戶總覽	(n.) account summary
通知	(n.) notification
勞動保障卡	(n.) labor protection card

AUTOMATED BANKING
自動化銀行業務

▸ 中文	▸ 英文
插入(卡片)	(v.) insert = put in
提款機的顯示螢幕	(n.) screen of the ATM
晶片卡	(n.) IC card = smart card = chip card = chipped card (口語) = chip-and-PIN card
晶片卡讀卡機	(n.) smart card reader
晶片密碼	(n.) chip PIN
智慧型手機	(n.) smart phone
登記；進入	(n.) entry
登錄	(v.) login (和介系詞to搭配) = log in = log on
硬幣分類機	(n.) coin sorter
虛擬鍵盤	(n.) virtual keyboard

AUTOMATED BANKING
自動化銀行業務

▶ 中文	▶ 英文
傳真交易指示	(n.) general facsimile instruction = fax banking
傳真機	(n.) fax machine
號碼牌	(n.) number slip
補(鈔)	(v.) restock
補發卡片	(n.) card replacement
補摺機	(n.) passbook entry machine (PEM)
裝(鈔)	(v.) load
電子貨幣；電子錢	(n.) electronic money
電子認證	(n.) electronic authentication
電子錢包	(n.) electronic purse
電話銀行；電話語音銀行	(n.) phone banking
監視器	(n.) security camera
磁條	(n.) magnetic stripe

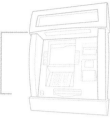

Automated Banking
自動化銀行業務

▸ 中文	▸ 英文
磁條卡	(n.) magnetic stripe card
網路ATM	(n.) online ATM = web ATM
網路下單	(n.) Internet trading
網路銀行；網銀	(n.) Internet banking = online banking = e-banking / E-banking = electronic banking = web banking = net banking / netbanking
網銀使用者代號	(n.) online banking user ID = online banking access ID
網銀密碼	(n.) online banking password
維修人員	(n.) repairman
銀行通路	(n.) banking channel

AUTOMATED BANKING
自動化銀行業務

▶ 中文	▶ 英文
領取(金融卡、存摺等)	(v.) collect
數幣機	(n.) coin-countering machine = coin rolling machine = coin counter
歷史交易明細	(n.) transaction history
螢幕選項提示	(n.) screen prompts = on-screen prompts
點鈔機	(n.) bill counter = banknote counter = money counter
簡訊銀行	(n.) text banking
轉帳功能	(n.) transfer function = transfer feature
轉盤密碼鎖;羅盤鎖	(n.) combination lock
轉盤組合密碼	(n.) combination
鎖卡(被鎖住的卡)	(n.) locked card

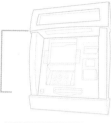

Automated Banking
自動化銀行業務

▶ 中文	▶ 英文
簽帳卡	(n.) debit card = check card
觸控螢幕	(n.) touch-sensitive screen = touch screen = touchscreen = touch panel
驗鈔機	(n.) currency detector = counterfeit currency detector = counterfeit bill detector = bill validator = bill acceptor

NOTE 筆記頁

外匯業務篇

FOREIGN EXCHANGE BUSINESS

FOREIGN EXCHANGE BUSINESS
外匯業務

▸中文	▸英文
(兌換外幣的)水單	(n.) exchange memo = exchange form
(匯出匯款的)受款人	(n.) beneficiary
(匯出匯款的)受款行	(n.) beneficiary bank
人民幣	(n.) Renminbi (CNY)
干預	(n.) intervention
日圓	(n.) Japanese Yen
代收行	(n.) collecting bank
外匯	(n.) foreign exchange (FX)
外匯干預	(n.) foreign exchange intervention
外匯存底	(n.) foreign exchange reserve
外匯行情表	(n.) foreign exchange quotations
外匯波動	(n.) foreign exchange fluctuation

FOREIGN EXCHANGE BUSINESS
外匯業務

▶ 中文	▶ 英文
外匯損失	(n.) foreign exchange loss
外匯轉帳交易	(n.) FOREX fund transfer
外幣;外幣幣別	(n.) foreign currency
外幣兌換	(n.) money exchange
申報	(v.) declare
申報;正式書面的告知	(n.) declaration
地下匯率	(n.) black market rate
收款行	(n.) receiving bank
收盤匯率	(n.) closing rate
西聯匯款	(n.) Western Union remittance
兌換	(n.) conversion
兌換;改變…信仰	(v.) convert = change = exchange
即期匯率	(n.) spot rate
受票銀行	(n.) drawee bank

FOREIGN EXCHANGE BUSINESS
外匯業務

▶ 中文	▶ 英文
官方匯率	(n.) official rate
押匯行	(n.) negotiation bank = negotiating bank
波動	(n.) fluctuation
法定貨幣；法幣	(n.) legal currency = legal tender = fiat currency
信用狀	(n.) letter of credit
信匯	(n.) mail transfer (M/T) = air mail remittance = remittance by air mail
保兌行	(n.) confirming bank
約定的外匯匯率	(n.) stipulated forex rate
美金	(n.) American dollar = US dollar
英鎊	(n.) British Pound (GBP) = Sterling Pound
面額	(n.) denomination

FOREIGN EXCHANGE BUSINESS
外匯業務

▸ 中文	▸ 英文
套匯匯率	(n.) arbitrage rate = cross rate
紐幣	(n.) New Zealand Dollar
釘住(某貨幣的匯率)；使…固定在	(v.) peg
國外匯款	(n.) foreign remittance
國際金融業務分行	(n.) Offshore Banking Unit (OBU)
強勢貨幣	(n.) hard currency
現鈔匯率	(n.) cash rate
票匯	(n.) demand draft (D/D) = remittance by demand draft = bill remittance
統一費率	(n.) flat rate
貨幣	(n.) currency
通知行	(n.) correspondent bank

FOREIGN EXCHANGE BUSINESS
外匯業務

▸中文	▸英文
通知銀行	(n.) notifying bank = advising bank
通匯銀行	(n.) correspondent bank
閉鎖貨幣	(n.) blocked currency
最新匯率	(n.) current rate
報價	(n.) quotation = quote
換匯	(n.) foreign exchange swaps
港元	(n.) Hong Kong Dollar
牌告匯率	(n.) nominal rate
牌告匯率	(n.) posted rate
結匯	(n.) foreign exchange settlement
買入價；買入匯率	(n.) buying rate
貶值；折舊	(n.) depreciation
開狀銀行	(n.) issuing bank = opening bank

FOREIGN EXCHANGE BUSINESS
外匯業務

▸ 中文	▸ 英文
開盤匯率	(n.) opening rate
匯入匯款	(n.) in-coming remittance = inward remittance
匯出匯款	(n.) out-going remittance = outward remittance
匯兌換算表	(n.) exchange table = conversion table
匯率	(n.) exchange rate = rate of exchange
匯率	(n.) conversion rate
匯率看板	(n.) exchange rate board
新加坡幣	(n.) Singapore Dollar (SGD)
新貨幣	(n.) new currency
瑞士法郎	(n.) Swiss Franc (CHF)
瑞典克朗	(n.) Swedish Krona (SEK)
補償銀行	(n.) reimbursing bank

FOREIGN EXCHANGE BUSINESS
外匯業務

▶ 中文	▶ 英文
電匯	(n.) telegraphic transfer (T/T) = cable remittance = remittance by cable
遠期外匯契約	(n.) currency forward
遠期匯率	(n.) forward rate
增值；升值	(n.) appreciation
歐元	(n.) Euro = Euro-currency
歐元區	(n.) eurozone
歐元體系	(n.) Eurosystem
歐盟	(n.) European Community
賣出價；賣出匯率	(n.) selling rate
澳幣	(n.) Australian Dollar
環球銀行財務電信系統	(n.) Society for Worldwide Interbank Financial Telecommunication (SWIFT)
讓購銀行	(n.) transferring bank

支票業務篇

CHECKING BANKING SERVICES

CHECKING BANKING SERVICES
支票業務

▶ 中文	▶ 英文
(支票)抬頭；付款行；受票人	(n.) drawee
(票據)可轉讓的	(adj.) negotiable
(票據)禁止背書轉讓的	(adj.) non-negotiable
不可轉讓支票	(n.) non-negotiable check
不記名支票	(n.) bearer check = check payable to bearer
支票	check
支票簿	(n.) checkbook
代收行	(n.) collecting bank
出納	(n.) cashier
可轉讓支票	(n.) negotiable check
可轉讓票據	(n.) negotiable instruments
外埠支票	(n.) domiciled check = out-of-state check = non-local check
本埠支票	(n.) local check

CHECKING BANKING SERVICES
支票業務

▸中文	▸英文
本票	(n.) promissory note (P/N)
兌現	(n.) encashment
即期匯票	(n.) sight bill = bill on demand
使…中止	(v.) suspend
受款人	(n.) payee
延後(付款)	(v.) defer
承兌	(n.) acceptance
拒付並退回；退(票)	(v.) bounce
空白支票	(n.) blank check
空頭支票；芭樂票	(n.) rubber check = bad check = dishonored check = bounced check
金錢	(n.) money
保付支票	(n.) certified check

CHECKING BANKING SERVICES
支票業務

▸ 中文	▸ 英文
約定好的	(adj.) promissory
背書	(v.) endorse
背書	(n.) endorsement
背書人;轉讓人	(n.) endorser
冥紙;紙錢	(n.) ghost money = hell money = paper money for ghosts = paper money for the dead
旅支(旅行支票)	(n.) traveler's check
記名支票	(n.) order check = check payable to order
託收;代收	(n.) collection
託收;徵(稅)	(v.) collect
退(票);拒付;不尊重	(v.) dishonor
偽造的假支票	(n.) forged check
商業本票	(n.) commercial paper (CP)

CHECKING BANKING SERVICES
支票業務

▸ 中文	▸ 英文
執票人	(n.) bearer = the bearer of the check = the holder of the check = check holder
現金；現鈔(不可數)；兌現	(n.) (v.) cash
票根；(支票)存根	(n.) check stub = counterfoil
票據；匯票	(n.) bill of exchange
票據交換	(n.) clearance
票據交換所	(n.) clearing house
票據託收	(n.) a bill for collection
尊榮；如期支付	(v.) honor
無效支票；作廢支票	(n.) voided check
無劃線支票；普通支票	(n.) open check
開空頭支票	(n.) check kiting
開空頭支票的人	(n.) kite-flyer

CHECKING BANKING SERVICES
支票業務

▸ 中文	▸ 英文
開票人；發票人	(n.) the drawer = the drawer of the check
毀損的支票	(n.) mutilated check
過期支票	(n.) out-of-date check
逾期匯票	(n.) overdue bill
電子旅支	(n.) e-traveler's check
劃線支票；平行線支票	(n.) crossed check
撤回(支票)	(v.) countermand
遠期支票	(n.) post-dated check
遠期匯票	(n.) distance bill = bill at distance
銀行支票	(n.) banker's check
銀行本票	(n.) cashier's check
複簽；副署；複簽	(v.) (n.) countersign
應付的	(adj.) payable
應付票據	(n.) bills payable

信用卡業務篇

CREDIT CARD BUSINESS

CREDIT CARD BUSINESS
信用卡業務

▸中文	▸英文
(信用卡的)簽名處	(n.) signature strip
(信用卡的)安全驗證碼	(n.) card verification code (CVC) = card verification value (CVV or CVV2) = card verification value code (CVVC) = card validation code = card security code (CSC) = security code number = verification code (v-code)
(保管箱的)租金;租用費用	(n.) rental fee = rent = rental
(租用保管箱的)保證金	(n.) security deposit
(商家發行的)簽帳卡	(n.) charge card

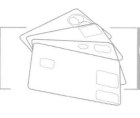

CREDIT CARD BUSINESS
信用卡業務

▸ 中文	▸ 英文
(電腦資料的)處理	(v.) process
VISA金融卡	(n.) VISA debit card
入帳日	(n.) posting day
口號	(n.) slogan
不動用信用卡循環額度的卡友	(n.) nonrevolver
分期付款	(n.) installment = hire purchase (HP) (英式英語)
月結對帳單	(n.) monthly statement
世界卡	(n.) world card
凸字信用卡	(n.) embossed credit card
卡友	(n.) card member
卡奴	(n.) credit card slave
卡債	(n.) credit card debt
卡號	(n.) credit card number

CREDIT CARD BUSINESS
信用卡業務

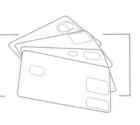

▶ 中文	▶ 英文
可用信用額度	(n.) available credit line = available credit limit
外債	(n.) external debt
失卡零風險	(n.) zero liability
失卡零風險	(n.) zero liability on lost card
本月應繳金額	(n.) new balance
未付餘額	(n.) outstanding balance
未到期的	(adj.) undue
未償付的；未清償的	(adj.) outstanding
申請	(v.) apply (和for連用)
白金	(n.) platinum (不可數)
白金卡	(n.) platinum card
交易；業務	(n.) transaction
回饋	(n.) reward
年費	(n.) annual fee

CREDIT CARD BUSINESS
信用卡業務

▸ 中文	▸ 英文
有效期限	(n.) valid date = validity date
有效期限	(n.) expiration date
自動加值	(n.) autoload
自動語音專線	(n.) automated hotline
兌換(紅利點數)	(v.) redeem
免付費電話	(n.) toll-free number
免費機票	(n.) complimentary air ticket
每週對帳單	(n.) weekly statement
刷(卡)消費；從(信用卡)扣款	(v.) charge
刷爆(信用卡)	(phr.) max out
法人；企業	(n.) corporation
法人的；企業的	(adj.) corporate
金融信用卡	(n.) combo card
附卡	(n.) supplementary card

CREDIT CARD BUSINESS
信用卡業務

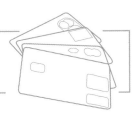

▶ 中文	▶ 英文
附卡持卡人	(n.) co-cardholder
信用卡	(n.) credit card
信用卡收單行	(n.) merchant bank
信用卡收單業務	(n.) merchant processing service
信用卡客服電話	(n.) credit card service line
信用卡對帳單	(n.) credit card statement
信用卡簽單	(n.) credit card slip
信用狀況;債務還款能力	(n.) credit standing
信用額度;刷卡額度	(n.) credit limit = credit line
保管箱	(n.) safe deposit box = custodial box = custodian box = coffer
客服人員	(n.) customer service representative

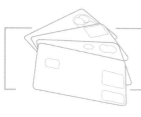

CREDIT CARD BUSINESS
信用卡業務

▶ 中文	▶ 英文
客服中心	(n.) customer service call center = call center
持卡人	(n.) cardholder
紅利點數	(n.) bonus points = reward points = points
美國運通卡	(n.) American Express Card
負債整合	(n.) debt consolidation
重新啟用;解除	(v.) reactivate
哩程數	(n.) air miles
討債	(n.) debt collection
討債公司	(n.) debt collection company
停用	(v.) deactivate = disable
側錄	(n.) skimming

CREDIT CARD BUSINESS
信用卡業務

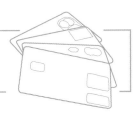

▸ 中文	▸ 英文
側錄機	(n.) skimmer
商家	(n.) merchant (可數名詞)
商務卡	(n.) commercial card
專員服務專線	(n.) manned hotline
御璽卡	(n.) signature card
悠遊卡	(n.) EasyCard
悠遊聯名卡	(n.) co-branded EasyCard
啟用；開啟	(v.) activate = enable
清償	(n.) clearance (n.) liquidation (phr.) pay off
清償證明	(n.) clearance certificate
現金卡	(n.) cash card
現金回饋	(n.) cash rebate = cash back
累積(紅利點數)	(v.) accumulate = amass

CREDIT CARD BUSINESS
信用卡業務

▸ 中文	▸ 英文
處理交易(手續)	(phr.) go through the formalities
備忘錄	(n.) memo
最低繳款金額	(n.) minimum payment
最後繳款日	(n.) payment due date
剩餘的；有空的	(adj.) available
剩餘額度	(n.) available credit
循環的	(adj.) revolving
循還利息	(n.) revolving credit interest
援助；協助	(n.) assistance
普卡	(n.) classic card
無凸字信用卡	(n.) un-embossed credit card
無限卡	(n.) infinite card
無限的	(adj.) infinite
發卡行	(n.) issuing bank

CREDIT CARD BUSINESS
信用卡業務

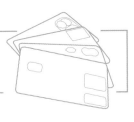

▸ 中文	▸ 英文
發行	(v.) issue
盜刷交易	(n.) fraudulent transactions
結算	(n.) settlement
結算日	(n.) settlement date
黑卡	(n.) Centurion card = the black card
鈦	(n.) titanium
鈦金卡	(n.) titanium card
債務	(n.) debt
債務人(欠錢的那一方)	(n.) debtor
債權人(借錢的那一方)	(n.) creditor = debtee
債權回收	(n.) debt recovery
催告信；催收函	(n.) dunning letter = collection letter
催討人員	(n.) debt collector

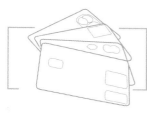

CREDIT CARD BUSINESS
信用卡業務

▸中文	▸英文
塑膠貨幣	(n.) plastic money
新創公司	(n.) start-up
經典的；典型的	(adj.) classic
補充的；附加的	(adj.) supplementary
道路救援	(n.) roadside assistance
違約	(n.) delinquency
違約；違約	(n.) (v.) default
過期；滿期	(v.) expire
過期的	(adj.) overdue
電子對帳單	(n.) e-statement = E-statement = electronic statement = paperless statement = online statement = non-physical statement
電話銀行專員	(n.) telephone banking agent
零利率分期付款	(n.) zero fee installment purchase

CREDIT CARD BUSINESS
信用卡業務

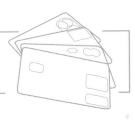

▶ 中文	▶ 英文
預借現金	(n.) cash advance
預借現金手續費	(n.) cash advance fee
預借現金額度	(n.) cash advance line
墊款	(n.) advance
對帳單	(n.) statement
滿期;到期	(n.) expiration
滯納金	(n.) default penalty fee
語音提示	(n.) voice prompt
認同卡(如台灣銀行發行的導盲犬認同卡)	(n.) affinity card
酷幣卡;禮物卡	(n.) gift card = prepaid card = charge card
銀聯卡	(n.) Union Pay Card
寬限期	(n.) grace period = days of grace
歐債危機	(n.) European debt crisis

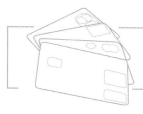

CREDIT CARD BUSINESS
信用卡業務

▶ 中文	▶ 英文
餘額代償	(n.) balance transfer
機場接送服務	(n.) airport pick-up service
機場貴賓室	(n.) airport VIP lounge
遲繳違約金	(n.) late payment fee
儲值卡	(n.) stored-value card = value card
聯名卡	(n.) co-branded card
禮券	(n.) gift certificate = gift token = gift voucher
簽帳日	(n.) transaction day
贈品	(n.) giveaway
關帳日	(n.) closing date

NOTE 筆記頁

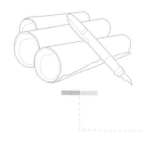

保險業務篇

INSURANCE BUSINESS

INSURANCE BUSINESS
保險業務

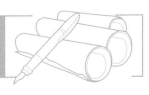

▸ 中文	▸ 英文
(保單的)解約金	(n.) cash value
(保單的)滿期	(n.) expiration
(保單的)滿期日	(n.) expiration date
(第三人)責任險	(n.) liability insurance = third party liability insurance
大眾捷運系統旅客運送責任保險	MRT passengers liability insurance
不分紅保單	(n.) nonparticipating policy
不可抗力	(n.) Force Majeure
不實說明	(n.) misrepresentation
公共意外責任保險	public liability insurance
代辦手續費	(n.) agency commission
仲裁	(n.) arbitration
任意險	(n.) optional insurance = voluntary insurance
再保險	(n.) reinsurance
年金保險	(n.) annuity insurance

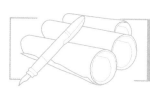

INSURANCE BUSINESS
保險業務

▶ 中文	▶ 英文
自負額	(n.) deductible = out-of-pocket cost
住宅火災及地震基本保險	residential fire & basic earthquake insurance
免責條款	(n.) escape clause
告知	(n.) declaration
批單	(n.) endorsement
投保期間	(n.) policy term = insurance term
投資型保單	(n.) investment-oriented insurance
汽車車體險	motor physical damage insurance
汽車定率自負額保險	motor fixed rate deductible insurance
汽車附加險	motor insurance extended coverage
汽車強制險	compulsory automobile liability insurance
汽車第三人責任險	motor third party liability insurance

INSURANCE BUSINESS
保險業務

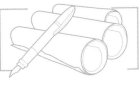

▸ 中文	▸ 英文
汽車竊盜損失保險	motor theft loss insurance
足額保險	(n.) full value insurance
車損險	(n.) physical direct damage insurance
車碰車	(n.) car collision
車險	(n.) automobile insurance = car insurance
受益人	(n.) beneficiary
受託人	(n.) fiduciary = trustee = consignee
定期保險	(n.) term insurance
承保範圍	(n.) coverage
拒保	(n.) declination
附加費用	(n.) expense loading
保代;保險代理人;保險業務員	(n.) insurance agent
保代公司	(n.) insurance agency

INSURANCE BUSINESS
保險業務

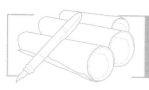

▸ 中文	▸ 英文
保全業責任保險	security guard liability insurance
保單;保險契約	(n.) policy
保單貸款;保單質借	(n.) policy loan
保費	(n.) premium = insurance premium
保經;保險經紀人	(n.) insurance broker
保險;保費;保險業	(n.) insurance
保險人(指保險公司)	(n.) insurer = insurance company
保險金額;保額	(n.) payout = insured amount = sum insured
保險賠付金;理賠金	(n.) indemnity = insurance money
要保人	(n.) applicant
要保書	(n.) application form = proposal

INSURANCE BUSINESS
保險業務

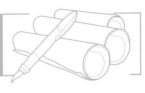

▸ 中文	▸ 英文
員工誠實保證保險	fidelity bond insurance
射倖契約	(n.) aleatory contract
旅平險	(n.) travel accident insurance
核保員;承銷公司	(n.) underwriter
索賠	(n.) (v.) claim
純保費	(n.) premium pure
退費	(v.) (n.) refund
除外責任附加條款	(n.) exclusion rider
高爾夫球責任險	golf liability insurance
健保費	(n.) health insurance premium
勘查;調查	(v.) survey
國民年金保費	(n.) national annuity insurance premium

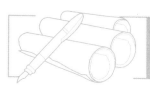

▸ 中文	▸ 英文
強制車險附加駕駛人傷害條款 (單一事故)	compulsory automobile liability insurance with driver's PA (Personal Accident or single accident) coverage
強制險	(n.) compulsory insurance
強迫推銷	(n.) hard sell
產物金融業保管箱責任保險	safe deposit box liability insurance
產物保險	(n.) property and casualty insurance
產品責任保險	product liability insurance
第三人責任險慰問保險金附加條款	third party liability with solatium coverage
終生壽險	(n.) whole life insurance
被保險人	(n.) policyholder = insurant = the insured
勞保費	(n.) labor insurance premium

INSURANCE BUSINESS
保險業務

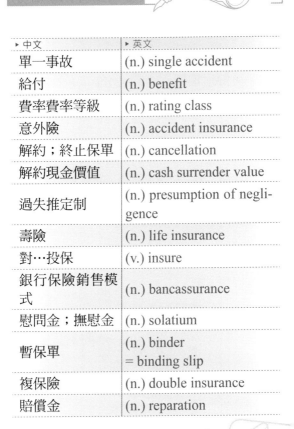

▸ 中文	▸ 英文
單一事故	(n.) single accident
給付	(n.) benefit
費率費率等級	(n.) rating class
意外險	(n.) accident insurance
解約;終止保單	(n.) cancellation
解約現金價值	(n.) cash surrender value
過失推定制	(n.) presumption of negligence
壽險	(n.) life insurance
對…投保	(v.) insure
銀行保險銷售模式	(n.) bancassurance
慰問金;撫慰金	(n.) solatium
暫保單	(n.) binder = binding slip
複保險	(n.) double insurance
賠償金	(n.) reparation

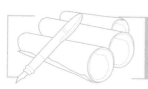

▶中文	▶英文
機車強制險駕駛人附加條款	compulsory motorcycle liability insurance with motorcyclist's personal accident coverage
應收帳款保險	accounts receivable insurance
營業中斷險	business interruption insurance
簡易郵政壽險	(n.) postal life insurance
續保保費	(n.) renewal premium
竊盜損失險	(n.) theft loss insurance
變額年金壽險	(n.) variable annuity insurance
變額萬能壽險	(n.) variable universal life insurance (VUL)
變額壽險	(n.) variable life insurance

NOTE 筆記頁

放款和理財業務篇

LOAN AND PERSONAL FINANCING SERVICES

LOAN AND PERSONAL FINANCING SERVICES
放款和理財業務

▶ 中文	▶ 英文
(利率的)加碼	(n.) markup
(利率的)減碼	(n.) markdown
(法規的)鬆綁	(n.) deregulation
(股票)賣空；做空；融券	(n.) short selling
(股票的)迴光反照	(phr.) dead cat bounce
(股票等)止跌回升；跌停看漲	(v.) bottom out
(基金的)申購	(v.) subscribe (和to搭配)
(基金的)申購；認購；訂購	(n.) subscription (和to搭配)
(基金的)績效	(n.) performance
(募集基金的)公開說明書	(n.) prospectus
(經濟的)崩盤；瓦解	(n.) meltdown = crash = collapse

LOAN AND PERSONAL FINANCING SERVICES
放款和理財業務

▶ 中文	▶ 英文
(銀行放款部的) 業務人員	(n.) Account Officer (AO)
(擔保品或抵押品的)回收	(n.) repossession
(擔保品或抵押品的)收回	(v.) repossess
(聯貸案的)主辦行	(n.) lead bank
一次清償貸款	(n.) bullet loan
下單筆	(n.) lump sum investment
子公司	(n.) subsidiary company
小額放款	(n.) microloan
不動產;房地產	(n.) real estate
中小企業	(n.) small and medium enterprises
公司債券;信用債券	(n.) debenture (英式英語)
公債	(n.) public bond
分散風險	(n.) risk diversification

LOAN AND PERSONAL FINANCING SERVICES
放款和理財業務

▶ 中文	▶ 英文
毛利	(n.) gross margin
主推商品	(n.) flagship product
主權基金;主權財富基金	(n.) sovereign wealth funds
付款	(n.) payment
代客操作	(n.) discretionary account operation
出席人數	(n.) turnout
可轉換公司債	(n.) convertible bond (CB)
巨額融資	(n.) jumbo financing
市占率	(n.) marketing share
市值	(n.) market capitalization = market cap
市場行銷	(n.) marketing
市場滲透率	(n.) market penetration
母公司	(n.) parent company
申購手續費	(n.) front-end load

LOAN AND PERSONAL FINANCING SERVICES
放款和理財業務

▸ 中文	▸ 英文
仲介；券商	(n.) brokerage
仲介公司	(n.) brokerage firm
企業放款	(n.) corporate loan
企業社會責任	(n.) corporate social responsibility (CSR)
企管碩士	(n.) Master of Business Administration (MBA)
共同基金	(n.) mutual funds
劣幣驅逐良幣	bad money drives out good
合併	(n.) merger
年利率	annual percentage rate (APR)
年終獎金；(保單的)分紅	(n.) bonus
成長收益型基金	(n.) growth & income fund
有利可圖的	(a.) lucrative
有形資產	(n.) tangible asset

LOAN AND PERSONAL FINANCING SERVICES
放款和理財業務

▸ 中文	▸ 英文
有毒資產	(n.) toxic asset
有擔保貸款	(n.) secured loan
次級房貸	(n.) subprime mortgage
次級貸款	(n.) subprime loan
次貸風暴	(n.) subprime meltdown = subprime crash = subprime crisis
老花眼鏡	(n.) presbyopia eyeglasses
考核	(v.) evaluate
行銷費用	(n.) promotion load
行銷話術	(n.) sales pitch
估價	(n.) appraisal
估價	(v.) appraise
占便宜	(phr.) take advantage
作業風險	(n.) operational risk
作業標準	(n.) operating standards
利潤	(n.) profit

▸中文	▸英文
抒困	(n.) bailout
投資	(v.) invest (和in搭配連用)
投資	(n.) investment
投資報酬率	(n.) return on investment (ROI)
投資環境	(n.) investment environment
投資顧問	(n.) investment consultant
投機客	(n.) speculator
每季	(phr.) each quarterly period
沖銷呆帳	(n.) charge-off
私募	(n.) private placement
赤字	(n.) red ink
併購	(n.) merger and acquisition (M&A)
併購	(v.) merge

LOAN AND PERSONAL FINANCING SERVICES
放款和理財業務

▶ 中文	▶ 英文
固定利率房貸	(n.) fixed-rate mortgage (FRM)
季	(n.) quarter
定期定額	(n.) dollar cost averaging (DCA) = dollar averaging = periodic investment = constant dollar plan = pound-cost averaging（英式英語）
房奴	(n.) mortgage slave
房仲；房地產經紀人	(n.) estate agent = real estate agent = realtor
房屋所有權狀	(n.) house title deed
房貸利率	(n.) mortgage rate
房貸抵押貸款證券	(n.) mortgage backed security (MBS)
房價	(n.) house price
承包商	(n.) subcontractor

▸ 中文	▸ 英文
抵押；擔保；房貸	(v.) (n.) mortgage
抵押品；擔保品	(n.) collateral
拖欠款 (在寬限期內的未償付款項)	(n.) arrears
放高利貸者	(n.) loan shark
法拍；法拍屋	(n.) foreclosure
炒房	(n.) land flips
股份有限公司	(n.) joint-stock company = stock company = incorporated company (Inc.) = publicly traded company
股東會	(n.) stockholders' meeting
股票	(n.) stock = share
股票上市	(n.) equity listing

LOAN AND PERSONAL FINANCING SERVICES
放款和理財業務

▶ 中文	▶ 英文
股票公開收購	(n.) takeover bid (TOB)
股票型基金	(n.) equity fund
股票面額；債券面值	(n.) par value = par = face value
股票操作	(n.) equity operations
股價	(n.) stock price = share price
股權	(n.) equity
花費	(v.) spend
金改；金融改革	(n.) financial reform
金磚四國	(n.) BRICs
金融界；金融業	(n.) financial industry = financial sector = financial circle = financial community
金融重建基金	(n.) financial restructuring fund
金融海嘯	(n.) financial tsunami

LOAN AND PERSONAL FINANCING SERVICES
放款和理財業務

099

▸ 中文	▸ 英文
金融商品	(n.) financial instrument = financial product
金融崩盤	(n.) financial collapse
金融超市	(n.) financial supermarket
金融監理	(n.) financial supervision
金融機構	(n.) financial institution
金融檢查	(n.) financial examination
非保本基金	(n.) non-capital guaranteed fund
信用	(n.) credit
信用違約交換	(n.) credit default swap (CDS)
信用緊縮	(n.) credit crunch = credit squeeze = credit withdrawal
信貸	(n.) personal loan
保本型基金	(n.) principal guaranteed fund
保證人	(n.) guarantor

LOAN AND PERSONAL FINANCING SERVICES
放款和理財業務

▸ 中文	▸ 英文
促銷	(n.) sales promotion
促銷活動	(n.) marketing campaign = promotional campaign
客戶開發經理	(n.) customer acquisition manager
封閉型基金	(n.) closed-end fund
帝寶	(n.) Palace Mansion
政府公債	(n.) government bond
流動性	(n.) liquidity
流動率；離職率；週轉率	(n.) turnover rate
洗錢	(n.) money laundering
盈餘	(n.) surplus
看不見的手	(n.) invisible hand
衍生性金融商品	(n.) financial derivatives = derivative financial instruments
風險	(n.) risk

▸ 中文	▸ 英文
風險承受;曝險	(n.) exposure (to risk)
個人理財專員	(n.) Personal Banker (PB)
哺乳室	(n.) lactation room
套利	(n.) arbitrage
展望	(n.) prospect
庫存	(n.) inventory
振興經濟方案	(n.) stimulus package
浪費	(v.) squander
消金	(n.) consumer credit
特別提款權	(n.) Special Drawing Rights (SDRs)
特許證;特許設立	(n.) (v.) charter
破產	(phr.) go bankrupt = go into bankruptcy = go bust = go under
能源股	(n.) energy equities

LOAN AND PERSONAL FINANCING SERVICES
放款和理財業務

▸ 中文	▸ 英文
衰退	(n.) recession
財力	(n.) financial strength
財力證明	(n.) proof of income
財政政策	(n.) fiscal policy
財務揭露	(n.) financial disclosure
配額	(n.) quota
除息	(n.) ex-dividend
高收益債券基金	(n.) high-yield bond fund
高利貸	(n.) usury
停滯	(n.) slowdown
停滯性通膨	(n.) stagflation
假處分	(n.) provisional injunction
區隔化；分級化	(n.) segmentation
商品	(n.) commodity
商譽；信譽	(n.) goodwill
國有化	(n.) nationalization

LOAN AND PERSONAL FINANCING SERVICES
放款和理財業務

▶中文	▶英文
國有化	(v.) nationalize
國庫券	(n.) treasury bill (T-Bill)
基金會	(n.) foundation
基金經理人	(n.) fund manager
基金認購手續費	(n.) fund subscription fee
基金贖回手續費	(n.) fund redemption fee
基準放款利率; 基本放款利率	(n.) prime rate
奢侈稅	(n.) luxury tax
推銷;推廣	(v.) promote
淨值	(n.) net asset value
理財	(n.) fund management = financial planning = wealth management = money management

LOAN AND PERSONAL FINANCING SERVICES
放款和理財業務

▸中文	▸英文
理專	(n.) financial consultant (FC) = financial advisor = financial planner = financial analyst
票息；優惠券	(n.) coupon
被套牢	(phr.) on the hook = be tied up
規範；規定	(n.) regulation
責任	(n.) liability
貨幣市場	(n.) money market
貨幣供給	(n.) money supply
貨幣政策	(n.) monetary policy
貨幣流通量	(phr.) money in circulation
貨幣貶值	(n.) devaluation
貧窮	(n.) poverty
通貨緊縮	(n.) deflation

▶ 中文	▶ 英文
通貨膨脹；通膨	(n.) inflation
連動債	(n.) structured notes
連帶保證人	(n.) surety
連帶保證責任	(n.) joint and several liability
頂尖理專	(n.) top financial consultant
備抵呆帳	(n.) allowance for doubtful debts = allowance for bad debts = allowance for nonperforming debts
創投基金	(n.) venture capital fund
報酬率	(n.) rate of returns
提前清償	(n.) prepayment = early repayment
提前清償違約金	(n.) prepayment penalty

LOAN AND PERSONAL FINANCING SERVICES
放款和理財業務

▶ 中文	▶ 英文
散戶	(n.) retail investor = private investor = small investor
期貨	(n.) futures
游資；閒置資金	(n.) idle money
減資	(n.) capital reduction
無形資產	(n.) intangible asset
無就業景氣型復甦	(n.) jobless recovery
無擔保貸款	(n.) unsecured loan
短期同業拆放市場	(n.) call market
稅	(n.) tax
善盡職守查帳；審慎評估	(phr.) do due diligence
貸款；放款	(n.) loan
貸款手續費	(n.) loan fee
貸款利率	(n.) lending rate

▸ 中文	▸ 英文
量化寬鬆	(n.) quantitative easing
開放型基金	(n.) opened-end fund
債券型基金	(n.) bond fund
債權債券憑證	(n.) collateralized debt obligation (CBO)
新興市場	(n.) emerging markets
業務(員)	(n.) sales representative = representative = rep
業務拜訪	(n.) sales call
業績	(n.) earnings = business performance
準備金；零用錢	(n.) allowance
資本適足率	(n.) capital adequacy ratio
資本額	(n.) capitalization
資訊不對稱	(n.) asymmetric information = asymmetry of information

LOAN AND PERSONAL FINANCING SERVICES
放款和理財業務

▶中文	▶英文
資訊揭露	(n.) information disclosure
資產報酬率	(n.) return on assets (ROA)
跨售;共同行銷	(n.) cross-selling
道德風險	(n.) moral hazard
道德勸說	(n.) moral suasion
違約金	(n.) breach penalty
違約風險	(n.) default risk
逾放比	(n.) non performing loan ratio
逾期放款	(n.) non performing loan (NPL) = overdue loan
電話行銷;直效行銷	(n.) telemarketing
境外基金	(n.) overseas funds
旗艦分行	(n.) flagship branch
旗艦店	(n.) flagship store

LOAN AND PERSONAL FINANCING SERVICES
放款和理財業務

▸ 中文	▸ 英文
槓桿(比率)	(n.) leverage = gearing (英式英語)
監察機構	(n.) watchdog
認股權	(n.) stock option
豪宅稅	(n.) Luxury Home Tax
銀行團	(n.) syndicate
銀行融資	(n.) bank financing
增資	(n.) recapitalize
履約保證	(n.) performing bond
撥款	(n.) grant
標售；拍賣	(n.) (v.) auction
歐豬五國	(n.) PIGS
熱錢	(n.) hot money
獎勵金	(n.) incentive award
課稅	(n.) taxation
銷售通路	(n.) distribution channel
餘額不足	(n.) insufficient funds

LOAN AND PERSONAL FINANCING SERVICES
放款和理財業務

▶ 中文	▶ 英文
擔保品;保證金	(n.) security
擔保債權憑證	(n.) collateralized debt obligation (CDO)
機動利率房貸;指數型房貸	(n.) variable-rate mortgage = adjustable rate mortgage (ARM)
蕭條	(n.) depression
融資;財金;金融	(n.) finance
選擇權	(n.) option
錄音	(v.) record
頭期款	(n.) down payment = initial installment
償還本金	(n.) repayment of principal
營業額;成交量;(籃球比賽的)失誤	(n.) turnover
績優股;藍籌股	(n.) blue chip stock

LOAN AND PERSONAL FINANCING SERVICES
放款和理財業務

▶中文	▶英文
總費用年百分率	annual percentage rate of total finance charges
聯貸	(n.) syndicated loan
避險；避險工具；對沖	(n.) hedge
避險基金；對沖基金；套利基金	(n.) hedge funds
還款	(n.) repayment
藍海策略	(n.) blue ocean strategy
轉介	(n.) referral
轉介	(v.) refer
壟斷；獨占	(v.) monopolize
龐氏騙局；老鼠會	(n.) Ponzi scheme = pyramid scheme
證券	(n.) securities
贈與稅	(n.) gift tax
關係企業貸款	(n.) affiliated lending

LOAN AND PERSONAL FINANCING SERVICES
放款和理財業務

▶ 中文	▶ 英文
競標	(n.) competitive bidding = bidding war
顧問	(n.) consultant
攤銷；(向銀行貸款的)本金分期償還	(n.) amortization = amortisation(英式英語)
攤還；(向銀行貸款的)分期償還	(v.) amortize
贖回手續費	(n.) redemption fee = back-end load

附錄 APPENDIXES

> **in the beginning** 首先
  = to begin with
  = to start with
  = in the first place
  = first
  = first and foremost
  In the beginning God created the heavens and the earth.
  起初，神創造天地。

> **moreover** 此外
  = furthermore
  = in addition
  = additionally
  = what is more
  = also
  = plus
  Moreover, the customer does not know how to use the ATM. He needs your help.
  此外，這位客戶不知如何使用自動櫃員機。他需要你的幫助。

> **besides** 更何況；況且

> **as a rule** 一般而言
  = at large
  = by and large
  = generally speaking

TRANSITION WORDS IN BANKING ENGLISH
附錄一 銀行口語常用轉承語

= generally
As a rule, working at a bank is not easy.
一般而言，在銀行工作不輕鬆。

» **to tell the truth**　事實上
= in fact
= in actuality
= in reality
= as a matter of fact
= actually
To tell you the truth, I am broke.
事實上，我破產了。

» **on the whole**　大體而言
= for the most part
= overall
= all in all
= on the average
On the whole, we did a good job.
大體而言，我們表現不錯。

» **to put it briefly**　簡而言之；簡單說
= in short
= in a word
= simply put
Simply put, you are fired.
簡單說，你被開除了。

TRANSITION WORDS IN BANKING ENGLISH

附錄一 銀行口語常用轉承語

> **for example** 舉例來說
> = for instance
> = take N for example
> = take N for instance
>
> You should be a good boy. **For example**, you should not bully your younger sister.
> 你應該做一個好男孩。例如說，你不應該欺負你的妹妹。

> **however** 然而
> = nevertheless
> = nonetheless
>
> I expected to make a lot of money. **However**, I lost all my money in the end.
> 本來我期待賺很多錢。然而，我最終失掉我所有的錢。

> **namely** 也就是說；換句話說
> = in other words
> = that is to say
> = that is
>
> The bank decided to hire me. **That is**, I got a job at a bank.
> 銀行決定僱用我。也就是說，我得到一份在銀行的工作。

> **by the way** 順便一提

TRANSITION WORDS IN BANKING ENGLISH

附錄一 銀行口語常用轉承語

= incidentally

By the way, the ATM is out of service for the time being.

順便一提,這臺自動櫃員機暫停服務。

» **in conclusion**   總結來說;總而言之

= in summary

= to conclude

= to sum up

= to summarize

To conclude, online banking is very convenient.

總而言之,網路銀行很方便。

» **thus**   因此

= therefore

= as a consequence

= as a result

= in consequence

= consequently

The teller is so beautiful. **Therefore**, many men tried to ask her out.

這銀行櫃員很美麗。因此,有很多男人曾試著約她出去。

BANKING DEPARTMENT AND FINANCIAL INSTITUTION
附錄二 銀行各部門和重要機構

營業部	business department
人資部	personnel department = human resource department
國外部	foreign department = international banking department
資訊部	information service department
信託部;(銀行的)信用部	trust institution = trust department = credit department
分行	branch
分行代碼;分行代號	branch code
銀行代碼;銀行代號	bank code
分公司	branch office
通訊處	correspondence office
金融控股公司;金控	financial holding company
投信公司	securities investment trust corporation

投顧公司	securities investment consulting corporation = securities investment advisory corporation
金管會	the Financial Supervisory Commission (FSC)
銀行局	Banking Bureau
證券期貨局	Securities and Futures Bureau
保險局	Insurance Bureau
檢察局	Financial Examination Bureau
聯徵中心	Joint Credit Information Center
聯準會；美聯儲	Federal Reserve Board (Fed)
銀行公會	The Bankers Association of the Republic of China (BAROC)
中央存款保險公司	Central Deposit Insurance Corporation (CDIC)
台灣金融研訓院	Taiwan Academy of Banking and Finance
票券金融公司	Bills Finance Companies

證券金融公司	Securities Finance Companies
國際清算行	Bank for International Settlements (BIS)
(臺灣)中央銀行	Central Bank of the Republic of China (Taiwan)
中央存款保險公司	Central Deposit Insurance Corporation
臺灣銀行	Bank of Taiwan
土地銀行	Land Bank of Taiwan
合作金庫	Taiwan Cooperative Bank
第一商業銀行	First Commercial Bank
華南商業銀行	Hua Nan Commercial Bank
彰化銀行	Chang Hwa Commercial Bank
上海商銀	Shanghai Commercial and Savings Bank
台北富邦銀行	Taipei Fubon Commercial Bank
國泰世華銀行	Cathay United Bank
兆豐銀行	Mega Bank
陽信銀行	Sunny Bank
元大銀行	Yuanta Commercial Bank

BANKING DEPARTMENT AND FINANCIAL INSTITUTION

附錄二 銀行各部門和重要機構

永豐銀行	Bank SinoPac
玉山銀行	E. Sun Bank
台新銀行	Taishin International Bank
臺灣新光商業銀行	Taiwan Shin Kong Commercial Bank
大台北銀行	Bank of Taipei
中國信託	Chinatrust Commercial Bank
臺灣企銀	Taiwan Business Bank
萬泰銀行	Cosmos Bank
華泰銀行	Hwatai Bank
大眾銀行	Ta Chong Bank
京城銀行	King's Town Bank
聯邦銀行	Union Bank of Taiwan
誠泰銀行	Macoto Bank
慶豐銀行	Chinfon Bank
遠東國際商銀	Far Eastern International Bank
大眾銀行	TC Bank
安泰商業銀行	Entie commercial Bank
日盛銀行	Jih Sun International Bank
華僑銀行	Bank of Overseas Chinese

花旗(臺灣)	Citibank Taiwan
星展銀行	Development Bank of Singapore (DBS)
匯豐銀行	Hongkong Shanghai Banking Corporation (HSBC)
渣打銀行	Standard Chartered Bank
農業金庫	Agricultural Bank of Taiwan
農會	Credit Departments of Farmers' Associations
漁會	Credit Departments of Fishermen's Associations
人壽保險公司	Life Insurance Companies
產物保險公司	Property and Casualty Insurance Companies
兩岸經濟合作架構協議	the Economic Cooperation Framework Agreement (ECFA)
備忘錄	Memorandum for Understanding (MOU)
國際貨幣基金	International Monetary Fund (IMF)
美國銀行	Bank of America (BOA)
雷曼兄弟	Lehman Brothers

附錄二 銀行各部門和重要機構

美國國際集團	American International Group (AIG)
友邦保險	American International Assurance (AIA)
高盛集團	Goldman Sachs
美林銀行	Merrill Lynch
摩根史坦利	Morgan Stanley
貝爾斯登	Bear Stearns
房利美	Fannie Mae
房地美	Freddie Mac
信評機構	Credit Rating Agency
穆迪投資顧問	Moody's Investors Service
標準普爾	Standard and Poor's (S&P)
惠譽國際信評	Fitch Ratings

CUSTOMER SERVICE CALL NUMBER

附錄三 各銀行客服電話

臺灣銀行	0800-000-258 0800-025-168	02-23758119
上海商銀	0800-003-111 0800-050-111	02-2391-1111
星展銀行	0800-808-889	02-6612-9889
土地銀行	0800-282-099 0800-089-369	02-23612543
匯豐銀行	0800-000098	02-8072-3000
彰化銀行	0800-365-889 0800-021-268	02-8181-2933
國泰世華	0800-818-001	02-2383-1000
渣打銀行	0800-051-234	02-4058-0088
遠東商銀	0800-231-788	02-8073-1166
花旗銀行	0800-012-345	02-2576-8000
台新銀行	0800-023-123 0800-000-456 0800-888-800 0800-085-858	02-2655-3355
元大銀行	0800-688-168	02-2182-1988
中國信託	0800-024-365 0800-001-234 0800-000-685	02-2745-8080

CUSTOMER SERVICE CALL NUMBER

附錄三 各銀行客服電話、

台北富邦	0800-007-889 0800-008-222 0800-099-799	02-8751-1313
兆豐商銀	0800-056-868	02-8982-0000
大眾銀行	0800-020-608 0809-028-888	07-9651988#2
第一銀行	0800-052-888	02-2173-2999
玉山銀行	0800-301-313	02-2182-1313
華南銀行	0800-231-039	02-2181-0101
永豐銀行	0800-058-888	02-2505-9999
新光銀行	0800-081-108	02-2171-1055
日盛銀行	0800-860-888 0800-212-255	(02) 2923-7288
萬泰銀行	0800-037-777	02-8023-9088
合作金庫	0800-033-175	04-2227-3131
陽信銀行	0800-085-134	02-2822-0122

註：由於各銀行近年來想減縮成本，因此不少銀
　　行慢慢取消0800免付費電話，或是砍掉可用
　　手機打的0800免付費電話，甚至在信用卡或
　　是網站也把免付費電話給移除。因此筆者這
　　裡提供讀者各銀行及信用卡的客服專線，如
　　遭移除，請多見諒，書中提供的各銀行客服
　　電話僅供讀者參考，實際請依照各銀行的揭
　　露為準。

DAILY SENTENCE IN BANKING ENGLISH

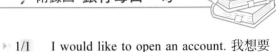

附錄四 銀行每日一句

- » 1/1 I would like to open an account. 我想要開戶。

- » 1/2 Please complete this application form. 請填寫這張申請表。

- » 1/3 Please check the amount before you leave the counter. 離開櫃臺前請確認金額。

- » 1/4 When will I get the credit card? 我什麼時候會拿到信用卡？

- » 1/5 I'd like to withdraw money from my account. 我想要從我的戶頭領錢。

- » 1/6 How much do you charge for the remittance? 你匯款手續費收多少？

- » 1/7 Could you tell me my balance? 能否把餘額告訴我？

- » 1/8 I suggest you open a current account. 我建議你開活期存款戶頭。

- » 1/9 Your balance at the bank is 30000 NT dollars. 你在本行的餘額是新臺幣三萬元。

- » 1/10 Sorry, the authorities concerned prohibits this kind of transaction. 抱歉，有關當局禁止這種交易。

- » 1/11 Sorry, it is against the bank's policy. 抱

歉，這違反銀行規定。

- ＞ 1/12　Please pass me your passbook. 請給我您的存摺。

- ＞ 1/13　The savings account carries interest of 1%. 活儲有1%的利息。

- ＞ 1/14　I would like to deposit 30000 into my account. 我想要存三萬到我的戶頭。

- ＞ 1/15　Please write down your account number. 請寫下您的帳號。

- ＞ 1/16　Please fill the remittance slip. 請寫一下匯款條。

- ＞ 1/17　Could I have your ID card? 可以把身分證給我一下嗎？

- ＞ 1/18　How much would you like to deposit into your account today? 您今天想要存多少錢？

- ＞ 1/19　The amount I want to credit my account is 10 thousand dollars. 我要存入的金額是一萬元。

- ＞ 1/20　How much is the interest rate? 利率是多少？

- ＞ 1/21　You cannot cash a crossed check directly. 你無法直接兌現劃線支票。

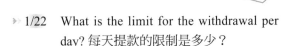

- 1/22　What is the limit for the withdrawal per day? 每天提款的限制是多少？

- 1/23　Could you put your signature here? 你可以簽在這裡嗎？

- 1/24　It is the bank's regulation. 這是銀行的規定。

- 1/25　Please input your PIN number. 請輸入您的密碼。

- 1/26　Your time deposit has not matured yet. 您的定存還沒有到期。

- 1/27　Will you please tell me whether you charge for checks? 請告訴我兌換支票要收手續費嗎？

- 1/28　You cannot cash this check right now. 你無法兌現這張支票。

- 1/29　I would like some change for these bills. 我想要把這些鈔票換成零錢。

- 1/30　You have to deposit this check into your account first. 你必須先把這張支票存到您的帳戶。

- 1/31　You can update your personal information through online banking. 你可以透過網銀更新個人資料。

DAILY SENTENCE IN BANKING ENGLISH
附錄四 銀行每日一句

» 2/1　I want to make an account with this bank. 我想要在這間銀行開戶。

» 2/2　Please fill out this form. 請填這張表格。

» 2/3　Could I get this bill in coins? 我可以把這張鈔票換成硬幣嗎？

» 2/4　The interest is added to your account every year. 每年的利息都加到你的存款中。

» 2/5　Please write down the amount you want to deposit. 請寫一下您要存的金額。

» 2/6　How much money do you want to credit with your account? 您想要存多少錢？

» 2/7　I'd like to close my savings account. 我要銷戶。

» 2/8　I need your signature at the back of this check. 我需要你幫我在支票後面背書。

» 2/9　What type of credit card would you like to apply for? 你想要辦什麼樣的信用卡？

» 2/10　When will I receive my ATM card? 我什麼時候可以拿到金融卡？

» 2/11　I want to make a withdrawal. 我想要提款。

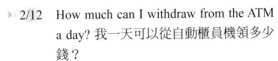

> 2/12　How much can I withdraw from the ATM a day? 我一天可以從自動櫃員機領多少錢？

> 2/13　I want to pay my gas bills by automatic bank transfer. 我想要透過自動轉帳來付我的瓦斯費。

> 2/14　What is the service charge for the remittance? 轉帳的手續費是多少？

> 2/15　How much of the remittance do you want to convert into Euro? 你要把多少匯款換成歐元？

> 2/16　Could I get a cash advance? 我能預借現金嗎？

> 2/17　You are overdrawn. 你透支了。

> 2/18　Tell me the current rate for Euro, please. 請告訴我歐元的即期匯率。

> 2/19　The interest rate for the savings account is 4%. 儲蓄存款的利率是4%。

> 2/20　Will you please cash this traveler's check? 請兌現這張旅行支票好嗎？

> 2/21　What kind of foreign currencies do you handle at your bank? 你們銀行有哪些外

幣？

> 2/22 Could you help me change this bill into coins? 你可以幫我把這鈔票換成零錢嗎？

> 2/23 I would like to take out a loan. 我要辦貸款。

> 2/24 Your deposit is exhausted. 你的存款領完了。

> 2/25 How much cash do you plan to deposit in your account? 你有多少錢要存入呢？

> 2/26 Please sign your name on the bottom line if you want to cash the check. 如果想兌現支票，請在底線上簽名。

> 2/27 Do you have a savings account in our bank? 你在我們銀行有戶頭嗎？

> 2/28 Here are your cash and passbook. 這是您的現金和存摺。

> 2/29 I would like to take out my mansion for a mortgage. 我想用我的豪宅來抵押借款。

DAILY SENTENCE IN BANKING ENGLISH

附錄四 銀行每日一句

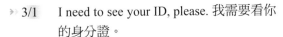

- » 3/1 I need to see your ID, please. 我需要看你的身分證。
- » 3/2 Please fill out this deposit slip. 請填這張存款條。
- » 3/3 Could I have this bill in coins? 我可以把這張鈔票換成零錢嗎？
- » 3/4 Can I cash a check at this bank? 我可以在這家銀行把這張支票兌現嗎？
- » 3/5 This credit card has been expired. 這張信用卡已經過期了喔。
- » 3/6 What is the going exchange rate? 現在的匯率是多少？
- » 3/7 You are over your credit limit. 你超過了你的信用額度。
- » 3/8 I want to use your automated billing system to pay my cell phone bills. 我想要用自動扣款來繳手機帳單。
- » 3/9 The bank applies an annual interest of 2%. 銀行採用2%的年利率。
- » 3/10 Here is your passbook. Keep it well and inform us whenever you lose it. 這是你的存摺。保管好存摺，遺失請通知我們。

DAILY SENTENCE IN BANKING ENGLISH

附錄四 銀行每日一句

- 3/11 Would you mind waiting for a moment? 您介意等一會兒嗎？

- 3/12 Could you please endorse this check? 可以請你在這張支票上背書嗎？

- 3/13 I would like to break this 1000 NT dollar note. 我想把這張一千元紙鈔換開。

- 3/14 Our minimum deposit for a savings account is 1000 NT dollars. 我們儲蓄存款的最低存款額是一千元新臺幣。

- 3/15 What is your selling rate for RMB yuan in notes now? 你們現在人民幣現鈔的賣價是多少？

- 3/16 Please wait a moment, I'll find out the rates of exchange for the Euro. 請等一會兒，我查一下歐元的匯率。

- 3/17 Your check has not matured yet. 你的支票尚未到期。

- 3/18 I want to close my account with you. 我想關掉在你們這裡的戶頭。

- 3/19 What kind of currency do you want? 你要哪種貨幣？

- 3/20 The password you just input is not correct.

DAILY SENTENCE IN BANKING ENGLISH

附錄四 銀行每日一句

您剛輸入的密碼不正確喔。

- ≫ 3/21 Would you like to draw money? 你今天要領錢嗎？
- ≫ 3/22 Here is your money. 這是您的錢。
- ≫ 3/23 I want to know whether I can cash a check here. 我想知道我能否在這裡兌換支票。
- ≫ 3/24 Please key in your passbook password. 請輸入您的存摺密碼。
- ≫ 3/25 Would you please try inputting another password? 請您再試別的密碼看看好嗎？
- ≫ 3/26 I want to deposit these checks in my daughter's account. 我想把這些支票存入我女兒的戶頭。
- ≫ 3/27 I forgot my account number. 我忘記我的帳號了。
- ≫ 3/28 I want to mortgage my mansion. 我想用我的豪宅來抵押。
- ≫ 3/29 You can set up automatic bill payments from this account. 你可以從這個帳戶設定自動扣款。

DAILY SENTENCE IN BANKING ENGLISH
附錄四 銀行每日一句

- 3/30 What kind of foreign currency do you want to change? 你要兌換哪種外幣？

- 3/31 Who can I call if I have technical problems in using online banking? 如果我在使用網銀碰到技術上的問題，我可以打給誰？

DAILY SENTENCE IN BANKING ENGLISH

附錄四 銀行每日一句

» 4/1   I want to close out my savings. 我要結清。

» 4/2   What's the interest rate right now? 現在的利率是多少？

» 4/3   What denominations would you like? 您要哪種面額的呢？

» 4/4   What's the current exchange rate? 現在的匯率是多少？

» 4/5   I want to apply for a credit card. 我想要辦信用卡。

» 4/6   I would like to make a deposit, please. 我想要存款。

» 4/7   Your credit card maxed out. 您的卡刷爆了。

» 4/8   I would like a loan against my house at Tianmu. 我想用我在天母的房子來擔保。

» 4/9   What's your selling rate for the Euro in notes today? 你們今天歐元現鈔的賣價是多少？

» 4/10   I want to put some money into my account. 我想要在我的戶頭存一些錢。

» 4/11   Please tell me what the annual interest rate

is. 請告訴我年利率是多少。

» 4/12 The PIN number you just input is not acceptable. 您剛輸入的密碼不正確。

» 4/13 May I have your passbook, please? 可以麻煩給我您的存摺嗎？

» 4/14 I would like to withdraw all my money from my account 我要把我存款全部提出來。

» 4/15 Please leave your name and telephone number. 請留下您的姓名和電話。

» 4/16 Please tell me your ID number. 您告訴我您的身分證字號。

» 4/17 Can you tell me the balance on my bank account? 你可以告訴我我的戶頭還有多少錢嗎？

» 4/18 Interest is paid at the rate of 1% per annum at present. 目前每年的利率是1%。

» 4/19 I lost my passbook. 我的存摺遺失了。

» 4/20 Please show me your passport. 請給我看您的護照。

» 4/21 What is the name of the remittee bank? 匯入行是哪一家銀行？

» 4/22 Have you brought your ID card as well as

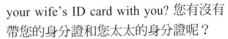

your wife's ID card with you? 您有沒有帶您的身分證和您太太的身分證呢？

- 4/23 I cannot recall my account number. 我沒有辦法想起我的帳號。

- 4/24 I want to remit some money to Korea. 我想要匯款到韓國。

- 4/25 How much do you charge for the exchange? 你們外幣兌換收多少手續費？

- 4/26 I want to convert the money into the Euro. 我想要換歐元。

- 4/27 How long will it take to approve my loan application? 批准我的貸款要多久時間？

- 4/28 Can I still make a transfer now? 我現在還可以匯款嗎？

- 4/29 You have a balance of 100 thousand NT dollars. 你的帳戶還有十萬元的餘額。

- 4/30 The annual fee is reasonable. 這年費不貴。

DAILY SENTENCE IN BANKING ENGLISH

附錄四 銀行每日一句

> 5/1　How would you like your money? 要哪種面額的呢？

> 5/2　There is no extra service charge. 我們不收額外的手續費。

> 5/3　You have exceeded your credit limit. 你已經超過你的信用額度了。

> 5/4　I would like to apply for a mortgage on my mansion. 我想用我的豪宅來抵押。

> 5/5　I lost my credit card. 我搞丟我的信用卡了。

> 5/6　The remittance that you just inquired about has not arrived yet. 您剛詢問的匯款還沒有匯進來。

> 5/7　What kind of credit card do you hold? 您持什麼樣的卡？

> 5/8　How much do you want to change? 您想要換多少錢？

> 5/9　You can make withdrawals at any ATM. 您可以用自動櫃員機來領錢。

> 5/10　Why don't you apply for the Internet banking? 您為什麼不申請網路銀行呢？

> 5/11　The bank can advance some money for

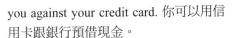

you against your credit card. 你可以用信用卡跟銀行預借現金。

» 5/12　Please write it in numbers. 請用小寫數字來填寫。

» 5/13　Your deposit is used up. 您的存款用完了。

» 5/14　I would like to close my account . 我想要銷戶。

» 5/15　You have to make a monthly payment. 你必須每月付款。

» 5/16　What is the exchange rate for Hong Kong dollars? 兌換港幣的匯率是多少？

» 5/17　I want to apply for a supplementary card. 我想要辦一張副卡。

» 5/18　Your loan has been past due for a while. 您的貸款已逾期未繳一段時間了。

» 5/19　The interest rate will go down again. 利率還會再降。

» 5/20　I would like to apply for a housing loan. 我想要辦房貸。

» 5/21　Will the interest rate go up? 利率何時會再上升？

DAILY SENTENCE IN BANKING ENGLISH
附錄四 銀行每日一句

- 5/22   I want to convert the money into the US dollars. 我想要把錢換成美金。

- 5/23   Your check cannot be cashed because it has not matured yet. 您的支票無法兌現，因為它還沒有到期。

- 5/24   When the money arrives, I will give you a call. 當錢入帳時，我會打電話通知。

- 5/25   Please write down your purpose of the loan. 請您寫下你辦貸款的目地。

- 5/26   We will inform you when the time deposit matures. 當定存到期，我們會通知您。

- 5/27   Would you please show me your exchange memo? 請您出示水單好嗎？

- 5/28   There is an error here. Please fill in another one. 這裡填錯了。請重填另一張。

- 5/29   We need to look into your credit standing. 我們需要查聯徵。

- 5/30   The maximum amount for the loan is eight million dollars. 最多可貸八百萬元。

- 5/31   How to apply for phone banking? 如何申請電話語音銀行？

DAILY SENTENCE IN BANKING ENGLISH

附錄四 銀行每日一句

- 6/1 What is the fee for the exchange? 這項兌換的手續費收多少？

- 6/2 Do you want to apply for a cash card? 你想要辦一張現金卡嗎？

- 6/3 What is the going interest rate of your bank for the loan? 你們這家銀行的貸款利息是多少？

- 6/4 May I ask the reason for your remittance? 我能問一下您匯款的原因嗎？

- 6/5 Please fill out this form in English. 請以英文來填寫這張表單。

- 6/6 Can I rent a safe deposit box here? 這裡可以租借保管箱嗎？

- 6/7 You can use the Internet banking anytime. 你可以隨時使用網銀。

- 6/8 The ATM kept my ATM card. 自動櫃員機吃掉我的卡了。

- 6/9 The ATM will retract the card if you input wrong PIN entry three times in a roll. 如果您連續輸入三次密碼錯誤，自動提款機會吃掉你的卡。

- 6/10 What is the lending rate? 貸款利率是多

少？

- 6/11 I have a payroll account with your bank. 我的薪資戶是你們這家銀行的。

- 6/12 Is the exchanged rate fixed? 匯率是固定的嗎？

- 6/13 Would you tell me your monthly salary? 您方便告訴我您的每月薪資嗎？

- 6/14 The exchange rate are constantly changing. 匯率不斷的在變動。

- 6/15 The buying rate is 45 NT dollars per Euro. 買進匯率是每歐元四十五塊臺幣。

- 6/16 The selling rate is 28 NT dollars per US dollar. 賣出匯率是每美金二十八塊臺幣。

- 6/17 Please fill out the remittance form in triplicate. 請填寫這張一式三份的匯款單。

- 6/18 The interest rate varies from time to time. 利率隨時變動。

- 6/19 What is covered under this insurance? 這份保險有哪些是承保的？

- 6/20 E-banking offers 24-hour service. 網銀提供二十四小時的服務。

DAILY SENTENCE IN BANKING ENGLISH

附錄四 銀行每日一句

- ▸ 6/21　I would like to open a checking account.
  我想要開支存戶。

- ▸ 6/22　Sorry, you don't have sufficient funds on
  your account. 抱歉，你的帳戶上沒有足
  夠的錢。

- ▸ 6/23　Do you exchange foreign currency here?
  你們這裡能兌換外匯嗎？

- ▸ 6/24　The remittance takes three days by cable.
  電匯會花三天到達。

- ▸ 6/25　I will process it for you immediately. 我立
  刻為您辦理。

- ▸ 6/26　Can you tell me how to fill out the withdrawal form? 您可以告訴我如何填取款
  條呢？

- ▸ 6/27　You should take the exchange rate risk
  into account. 你應把外匯風險也考量進
  來。

- ▸ 6/28　Our bank does not offer this kind of transaction, so I suggest you go to other banks
  to ask them. 我們銀行沒有提供這類的
  服務，所以我建議您可以去其它家銀行
  問問看。

DAILY SENTENCE IN BANKING ENGLISH
附錄四 銀行每日一句

> 6/29　Please tell me how much your bank expects as a down payment. 請告訴我你們銀行希望我頭期款付多少？

> 6/30　I would like to redeem my time deposit. 我想要把我的定存轉到活儲。

DAILY SENTENCE IN BANKING ENGLISH
附錄四 銀行每日一句

- 7/1　My ATM card is stuck in the ATM. 我的提款卡被自動提款機吃卡了。

- 7/2　The interest rate will go up. 利率會往上升。

- 7/3　Do you think it is the right time to buy stock? 你認為現在是進場買股票的好時機嗎？

- 7/4　What is the insurance premium? 保費是多少？

- 7/5　How much do you plan to deposit this time? 您打算這次存多少？

- 7/6　The exchange rate fluctuates every day. 匯率每天都會變動。

- 7/7　Do you want to open an Euro account with our bank? 您想要在我們銀行開個歐元外幣戶嗎？

- 7/8　I want to buy some Renminbi. 我想要買人民幣。

- 7/9　Can you tell me the interest rate for a time deposit? 您可以告訴我定存的利率嗎？

- 7/10　Please keep your exchange memo. 請保管好您的水單。

DAILY SENTENCE IN BANKING ENGLISH

附錄四 銀行每日一句

- 7/11 Make sure you completely understand all the terms and conditions before you put your signature on the agreement. 在這份合約上簽名前，請確認您了解所有的條款。

- 7/12 How do you want your checks? 您想要什麼面額的支票？

- 7/13 Our bank provides USD, JPY, EUR, and HKD accounts. 我們銀行提供美元、日圓、歐元和港幣外幣戶頭。

- 7/14 This kind of insurance is tax-free. 這種保險是免稅的哦。

- 7/15 I requested the bank manager to waive the charge because I have been a valued customer. 我要求銀行經理免除我的手續費，因為我是一個重要的客戶。

- 7/16 I want to report my passbook lost. 我要掛失我的存摺。

- 7/17 The bank will charge you NT 600 dollars for the remittance fee. 銀行會跟你收六百元臺幣的匯款手續費。

- 7/18 The customer should visit the bank in per-

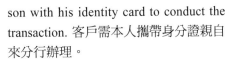

son with his identity card to conduct the transaction. 客戶需本人攜帶身分證親自來分行辦理。

> 7/19　Would you like to set up for internet banking? 您想要申辦網路銀行嗎？

> 7/20　Through text banking, you can send text messages to the bank to request information about your balances and recent transactions. 透過簡訊銀行，你可以透過簡訊向銀行查詢你的餘額和最近的交易明細。

> 7/21　You can access online banking at any time suitable to you. 你能在任何方便的時間使用網銀。

> 7/22　You can choose to renew the time deposit at maturity. 你可以在定存到期時選擇續存。

> 7/23　You can choose to redeem the time deposit at maturity. 你可以在定存到期時選擇轉到活儲。

> 7/24　The amount on a check must be the same in words and in numbers. 支票上的金額

在文字和數字上必須一樣。

» 7/25 The bank manager is at a meeting. 銀行經理在開會。

» 7/26 I would like to wire ten thousand NT dollars to my daughter. 我想要匯一萬元臺幣給我女兒。

» 7/27 How to set up the transaction password? 如何設定交易密碼？

» 7/28 Please contact your insurer if you have any question concerning the insurance policy. 如果你對這份保單有任何疑問，請你聯絡你的保險公司。

» 7/29 It is ten-yuan coin. 這是十元硬幣。

» 7/30 I would like to deposit some foreign currency into my account. 我想要把這些外幣存到我的戶頭。

» 7/31 What online services require a transaction password? 什麼樣的網路交易服務需要交易密碼？

DAILY SENTENCE IN BANKING ENGLISH

附錄四 銀行每日一句

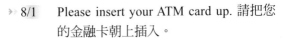

- » 8/1   Please insert your ATM card up. 請把您的金融卡朝上插入。

- » 8/2   May I ask the reason why you want to close your account with our bank? 我可以問您為什麼要關掉我們家的戶頭呢？

- » 8/3   I would like to open a USD account with your bank. 我想要在你們銀行開一個美金戶頭。

- » 8/4   Interest shall be calculated on the basis of a year of 365 days for New Taiwan Dollar deposits. 新臺幣存款之利息，依一年365天為基礎來計息。

- » 8/5   Sometimes interest rates rise and sometimes interest rates fall. It is hard to predict. 有時利率升，有時利率下降，這很難預測。

- » 8/6   My friend took out a loan with an interest rate of 2%. 我的朋友申請到利率2%的貸款。

- » 8/7   To open an account with most banks in Taiwan, you need to make a minimum deposit of 1,000 NT dollars. 在臺灣大部分

的銀行開戶，你需要至少存一千元新臺幣。

» 8/8　There will be an early withdrawal penalty if you withdraw money before the agreed-upon maturity date. 如果你在還沒有到期前就提款，就會有中途解約處罰。

» 8/9　The certificate of deposit has a 1-year maturity and a 6 percent fixed rate of interest. 這張定存單一年到期並有6%的固定利率。

» 8/10　After you filled out your withdrawl slip, then submit it to the teller. 在你填完你的取款條後，把它交給櫃員。

» 8/11　If you would like to open an account with this bank, we kindly ask you to fill out the form. 如果您想在這間銀行開戶的話，我們將請您填寫這份申請書。

» 8/12　During Lunar New Year holiday, most banks set the daily withdrawal limit between NT$100,000 and NT$150,000. 在春節期間，大部分的銀行設定每天最高提領限額在十萬到十五萬之間。

DAILY SENTENCE IN BANKING ENGLISH

附錄四 銀行每日一句

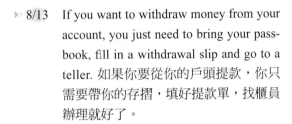

» 8/13 If you want to withdraw money from your account, you just need to bring your pass-book, fill in a withdrawal slip and go to a teller. 如果你要從你的戶頭提款，你只需要帶你的存摺，填好提款單，找櫃員辦理就好了。

» 8/14 This bank allows you to withdraw up to NT$100,000 a day from ATMs during Lunar New Year holiday. 這間銀行讓你在春節期間每天最高可提領十萬元。

» 8/15 This kind of banknote is not in circulation any more. 這種鈔票已不再流通了。

» 8/16 Don't take out an overdraft to buy any luxury. 不要動用透支來買任何奢侈品。

» 8/17 How long does it take for the remittance to arrive there? 匯款到那裡需要多少時間？

» 8/18 The agreement you filled out in the bank will be legally binding. 你在銀行填寫的同意書在法律上是有約束力的。

» 8/19 Since you have altered the amount in

words on the deposit slip, I have to make the deposit slip void. 因為你塗改了大寫數字的金額，所以我必須作廢這張存款條。

» 8/20 You should avoid overdrawing your account or your check. 你應避免戶頭透支或支票透支。

» 8/21 Your time deposit will mature two weeks later. 你的定存兩週後到期。

» 8/22 I want to renew my time deposit. 我想要定存展期。

» 8/23 You should know that there is some fee for early redemption. 你應知道中途贖回要收一些費用。

» 8/24 A balance of 10,000 NT dollars must be maintained in order to earn interest. 必須維持一萬元的餘額才能計息。

» 8/25 If you terminate your time deposit before maturity, you will forfeiting the promised interest. 如果你把定存提前解約，你會喪失約定好的到期利息。

» 8/26 Your credit card payments can be directly

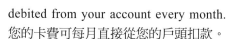

debited from your account every month. 您的卡費可每月直接從您的戶頭扣款。

» 8/27　Your signature on the withdrawal slip is not consistent with the specimen signature card at the bank. 你在取款條上的簽名和你在銀行留存的印鑑樣式並不一致。

» 8/28　If a time deposit is terminated prior to its scheduled maturity date, the interest payable on such deposit shall be calculated at a rate of 80% of the actual deposit tenors. 如果定存中途解約，應付利息將以實際的存期打八折計算。

» 8/29　Please hand over your valid passport. 請把你的有效護照遞給我。

» 8/30　This kind of coin is not in circulation any more. 這種硬幣已不流通了。

» 8/31　How far back can I view my account history? 我可以看到多久以前的帳戶歷史交易紀錄呢？

» 9/1 Don't forget to take back your ATM card. 不要忘記取出您的金融卡。

» 9/2 Please write down the amount both in words and in figures. 請用大寫數字和小寫數字寫下金額。

» 9/3 ATMs will retract the cash if you don't collected the cash within 30 seconds. 自動櫃員機會收回紙鈔，如果您未能在三十秒內領出。

» 9/4 Using an ATM is actually pretty easy. Just insert your ATM card and follow the on-screen prompts to conduct any transaction. 使用自動提款機很簡單。只要把你的金融卡插入並照著螢幕上的指示來做交易就行了。

» 9/5 The bank teller will inform you of the arrival of the transfer. 行員會通知你匯款進來了。

» 9/6 Please key in your 6 to 12-digit chip PIN. 請輸入您的六到十二位的晶片密碼。

» 9/7 Your passbook was demagnetized. 你的存摺被消磁了。

Daily Sentence in Banking English

附錄四 銀行每日一句

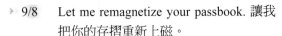

» 9/8 Let me remagnetize your passbook. 讓我把你的存摺重新上磁。

» 9/9 Please set a four-digit password for your magnetic stripe card. 請為您的磁條卡設一個四位數的密碼。

» 9/10 The payment is debited directly from your account. 這筆付款直接由你的帳戶扣款。

» 9/11 The card will be locked if the cardholder has entered the wrong PIN four times in a row. 如果持卡人連續輸入錯誤密碼達四次的話，卡片就會被鎖卡。

» 9/12 You may apply for an ATM card at any one of our branches where you can collect your ATM card. 您可以在任何一家你能來領取卡片的分行來申請金融卡。

» 9/13 Please print your name. 請用印刷體寫您的大名。

» 9/14 Please count your money in front of the teller. 鈔票請當面點清。

» 9/15 Harassing tellers is against the law. 騷擾行員是犯法的。

DAILY SENTENCE IN BANKING ENGLISH
附錄四 銀行每日一句

- 9/16 There have been a lot of telephone frauds, so please be careful. 最近有很多詐騙電話，因此請小心。

- 9/17 Do you deposit the money into your own account or into someone else's account? 請問您是把錢存進自己的戶頭還是別人的戶頭？

- 9/18 Please change your password of the ATM card at an ATM. 請在自動櫃員機上變更您的金融卡密碼。

- 9/19 Please insert your ATM card into the card slot and enter PIN. 請把你的金融卡插入卡的插口後，並且輸入密碼。

- 9/20 Replacement card will be issued immediately and should be received within 7-10 business days. 新卡會立即補發並應會在七到十個工作天之內拿到。

- 9/21 I want to have my ATM card replaced by the bank. 我想請銀行補發金融卡。

- 9/22 Do you want to activate the funds transfer function for your ATM card? 你想要啟用金融卡的轉帳功能嗎？

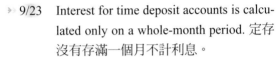

- 9/23   Interest for time deposit accounts is calculated only on a whole-month period. 定存沒有存滿一個月不計利息。

- 9/24   How do you like your money? 你想要哪種面額的呢？

- 9/25   Does this bank collect any service fee on checks? 這家銀行託收支票要收手續費嗎？

- 9/26   The bonus points accumulated on your card are lifelong available. 你刷卡累積的紅利點數一生都有效。

- 9/27   Every time you swipe your credit card to make a purchase, you collect reward points. 每次你刷卡消費，你就獲得紅利點數。

- 9/28   Woud you like to apply for the debit card function？ 你想要申請金融卡消費扣款的功能嗎？

- 9/29   After applying for the ATM card, the card will take 5-7 working days to arrive; in the meantime, you can conduct your banking over the counter at any branch. 在申請提

款卡後,需花五到七個工作天才會送
來。在此同時,你可以到任何一家分行
臨櫃辦理銀行交易。

> 9/30　You may choose to deactivate the third
party funds transfer or interbank funds
transfer if you do not want to make use of
the service. 如果你不想使用跨行匯款功
能,你可以選擇停用匯款給第三人的功
能。

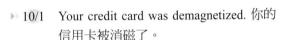

DAILY SENTENCE IN BANKING ENGLISH

附錄四 銀行每日一句

» 10/1   Your credit card was demagnetized. 你的信用卡被消磁了。

» 10/2   To reactivate a dormant account, you must go to the bank in person with your ID card as well as your Health IC card and fill out some application forms. 要解除靜止戶，你必須帶身分證和健保卡，本人親自到銀行辦理並填寫一些申請書。

» 10/3   Credit card skimming can occur easily in any place. 信用卡側錄很容易在任何地方發生。

» 10/4   It is vital for you to pay off the mortgage. 還清房貸對你來說是很重要的。

» 10/5   In what kind of denomination do you want your money? 您要什麼樣的面額？

» 10/6   Do you know the person you want to transfer your money to? 您匯錢的對象是您認識的嗎？

» 10/7   The remittance you asked about has not arrived yet. 您詢問的匯款還沒有到。

» 10/8   How much is the remittance? 要匯多少錢？

» 10/9 How much do you charge for the remittance? 辦理匯款要收多少手續費？

» 10/10 I would like to have a credit card from your bank. 我想要在貴行辦卡。

» 10/11 If you want to apply for a credit card, you must have a job and income. 如果您想辦張信用卡，您必須有份工作和收入。

» 10/12 If a customer schedules a recurring funds transfer and the payment date does not exist in a month, the payment will be processed on the last business day of that month. 如果客戶預約週期轉帳的日期並不存在於該月，則轉帳交易會在該月最後一個營業日處理。

» 10/13 The credit limit is usually raised or lowered depending on your previous years track record in terms of spending and repayment. 信用額度會按你前一年的刷卡消費和還款紀錄來調升或是調降。

» 10/14 You can earn cash rebate on your normal monthly spending. The cash rebate percentage guarantees 0.5% up to 6%. 你可以從你每月正常的消費中賺到現金回

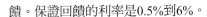

饋。保證回饋的利率是0.5%到6%。

» 10/15 This credit card pays a full 1% cash rebate on spending. 這張信用卡會給您購物1% 的現金回饋。

» 10/16 As long as you have a web-enabled cell phone, you can access your online banking account. 只要你擁有可以連到網路的手機，你就能登入你的網銀帳戶。

» 10/17 Here are your passbook and ID card. 這是您的存摺和身分證。

» 10/18 I am afraid that I cannot follow you. 我恐怕聽不懂您所說的。

» 10/19 Can I have your ID number? 能給我您的身分證字號嗎？

» 10/20 Can I have your bank account number? 能給我您的銀行帳號嗎？

» 10/21 You cannot cash your check because it is a crossed check. 您無法兌現此支票，因為這是劃線支票。

» 10/22 The PIN number is not acceptable. 密碼不對。

» 10/23 May I have your passport? 能給我您的護

照嗎？

- 10/24 Have a seat and wait a moment, please. 請坐並稍等一下。

- 10/25 Our bank does not provide foreign coin exchange service. 我們銀行不提供外幣的零錢兌換服務。

- 10/26 Do you already possess a credit card with our bank? 您已持有我們家的信用卡了嗎？

- 10/27 Can I advance 10,000 NT dollars against my credit card? 我可以用我的信用卡預借一萬元嗎？

- 10/28 Please keep the exchange memo carefully. 請保管好水單。

- 10/29 Do you want to rent a safe deposit box? 您要租保管箱嗎？

- 10/30 It requires your key and the bank's key to open a safe deposit box. 打開保管箱需要您的鑰匙跟銀行的鑰匙。

- 10/31 Our bank's credit card provide customers with a lot of benefits. 我們銀行的信用卡提供客戶很多優惠。

DAILY SENTENCE IN BANKING ENGLISH

附錄四 銀行每日一句

» 11/1   It doesn't matter. 沒關係。

» 11/2   It is not difficult at all to use the ATM. Let me show you how to make a time deposit. 使用自動櫃員機一點也不困難。讓我來示範如何辦理定存。

» 11/3   Could you tell me why you want to close your account? 您能告訴我銷戶的原因嗎？

» 11/4   I filled in the wrong amount. 我填錯金額了。

» 11/5   Do you have an account with our bank? 您在我們銀行有戶頭嗎？

» 11/6   You've filled in a wrong passport number. Please rewrite it. 您填的護照號碼不對，請重填。

» 11/7   The bank has to send a personal check to the drawee bank for collection. 銀行必須先把私人支票送到付款行去託收。

» 11/8   Will there be any charges to signing up for Internet Banking? 申辦網銀要收手續費嗎？

» 11/9   You can check your credit card account

balance, transaction history and reward points via Internet banking. 您可以透過網銀查詢您的信用卡帳戶餘額、交易紀錄和紅利點數。

» 11/10 Can I access my accounts through online banking when I am overseas? 當我人在國外時，我可以透過網銀使用我的帳戶嗎？

» 11/11 You can deposit cash via any ATM. 你可以透過任何一臺ATM來存款。

» 11/12 What are the criteria to open an account? 開戶要有什麼條件？

» 11/13 What are the required documentations to open an bank account? 開戶需要什麼證件？

» 11/14 How do I reactivate a dormant account? 我要如何才能解除靜止戶？

» 11/15 Buying the fund has a benefit of dispersing the risk. 買基金有分散風險的好處。

» 11/16 Please fill out and sign a safe-deposit box lease agreement. 請填寫並在這份保管箱租用同意書上簽名。

DAILY SENTENCE IN BANKING ENGLISH

附錄四 銀行每日一句

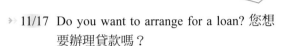

- 11/17 Do you want to arrange for a loan? 您想要辦理貸款嗎？

- 11/18 What is the lending rate? 貸款利率是多少？

- 11/19 I would like to change this banknote into coins. 我想要把這張鈔票換成零錢。

- 11/20 It takes about one week to collect this check. 託收這張支票需要一星期左右的時間。

- 11/21 How long does it take to collect the check? 託收這張支票要花多久？

- 11/22 Please leave your name and telephone number. 請留下您的姓名和電話。

- 11/23 What are the benefits of using Internet Banking? 使用網銀的好處有哪些？

- 11/24 To check your credit card account balance and transaction history via online banking, please select your credit card from the account summary. 為了透過網銀查詢您信用卡的餘額和歷史交易紀錄，請從「帳戶總覽」來選擇信用卡。

- 11/25 Can I redeem my credit card reward points

online? 我可以線上兌換我信用卡的紅利點數嗎？

» 11/26 Is Internet Banking available 24 hours? 網銀二十四小時都可以利用嗎？

» 11/27 It is the bank's policy. 這是銀行的規定。

» 11/28 How far back in record can I retrieve transactions for my credit card account via Internet Banking? 透過網銀，我可以取得我信用卡帳戶多久以前的交易紀錄？

» 11/29 You can change your ATM card PIN at any ATM. 您可以到任何一臺的ATM去變更金融卡密碼。

» 11/30 I think that the Euro is overvalued. 我認為歐元被過度高估。

DAILY SENTENCE IN BANKING ENGLISH
附錄四 銀行每日一句

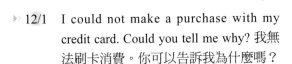

- 12/1 I could not make a purchase with my credit card. Could you tell me why? 我無法刷卡消費。你可以告訴我為什麼嗎？

- 12/2 What are the service hours of this bank? 銀行的服務時間是幾點？

- 12/3 Can I make a fund transfer any time of the day? 我能在一天的任何時間轉帳嗎？

- 12/4 Are there any exclusion from this insurance policy? 這張保單有沒有什麼不保事項？

- 12/5 What is the annual fee? 年費多少？

- 12/6 What should I do if I suspect that my password has been stolen or exposed to others? 如果我發現我的密碼被盜或是被洩露給別人時，我應該怎麼辦？

- 12/7 The headquarters of Bank of Taiwan is located in Taipei. 臺灣銀行的總行位在台北市。

- 12/8 I did not receive cash after making withdrawal through ATM, but my account was debited. What should I do? 在透過ATM提款後，我沒有拿到現金，但已從我帳戶扣款。我該怎麼辦？

- 12/9 What should I do if I am not able to login to Internet banking even if I have input the correct password? 即使我輸入正確的密碼我也無法登入網銀時，我該怎麼辦？

- 12/10 What should I do if I notice discrepancies on my accounts? 如果我發現我帳戶的交易紀錄不一致時，我該怎麼辦？

- 12/11 What if I'm disconnected from the Internet in the middle of a transaction? 如果我正在處理交易時，中途斷線該怎麼辦？

- 12/12 Is there any charge for making a fund transfer to a foreign country? 匯款到國外有任何的手續費嗎？

- 12/13 What do I need to do in order to activate the bank card for the first time? 我第一次開卡時需要做什麼？

- 12/14 My card is retained in an ATM. What should I do? 我的卡片被ATM吃卡了。我該怎麼辦？

- 12/15 What is the cash withdrawal (ATM) fee? 從ATM提款的手續費是多少？

- 12/16 Can you tell me where the nearest ATM

is? 你可以告訴我最近的ATM在哪嗎？

» 12/17 When will the beneficiary receive the money if I perform a fund transfer with other banks today? 若我今天在其它家銀行辦理匯款，收款人何時會收到款？

» 12/18 How to report loss or cancel an issued credit card? 我如何掛失或取消已發行的信用卡呢？

» 12/19 What is the interest rate for the savings account? 活儲的利率是多少？

» 12/20 What is the daily limit for cash withdrawal? 單日提款的限額是多少？

» 12/21 Is there cut-off time for bill payment? 繳款有截止時間嗎？

» 12/22 I want to know whether I can cash a check here. 我想知道我能否在這裡兌換支票。

» 12/23 There is no extra service charge. 我們不收額外的手續費。

» 12/24 Can I pay bills by my credit cards? 我能透過信用卡來繳付帳單？

» 12/25 You have to make a minimum deposit in

order to open a account. 您需要先存入一
筆存款才能開戶。

- 12/26 What are the advantages of doing tele-
graphic transfer online? 透過線上來辦電
匯有什麼優點？

- 12/27 Will I continue to receive paper statements
after subscribing to eStatement service?
在我申辦電子對帳單後，我仍然會繼續
收到紙本的對帳單嗎？

- 12/28 What precautions should I take when using public PCs for online banking? 當我
用公共電腦來上網銀時，我要採取什麼
預防措施？

- 12/29 How can I cancel my subscription to eS-
tatement service? 我要怎麼取消電子帳
單。

- 12/30 What if I have forgotten my Internet banking username or password? 如果我忘記
我網銀的帳號或密碼該怎麼辦？

- 12/31 You can receive OTP via your mobile
phone. 您可以透過手機收到您的動態密
碼。

NOTE 筆記頁

六 畫

七 畫

八 畫

189

十 一 畫

十 五 畫

十六畫

十 七 畫

十八畫

A

automatic queuing machine / 041
automatic renewal / 014
automobile insurance / 082
available / 073
available balance / 009
available credit / 073
available credit limit / 068
available credit line / 068

B

B2B / 040
back-end load / 112
bad check / 061
bad money drives out good / 093
bailout / 095
bait money / 032
balance / 002
balance check / 033
balance enquiry / 033
balance inquiry / 033
balance transfer / 077
bancassurance / 086
bank / 032
bank branch / 006
bank card / 043
bank charge / 008
bank clerk / 032
bank fee / 008

D

H

I

O

W

NOTE 筆記頁

NOTE 筆記頁

NOTE 筆記頁

NOTE 筆記頁

NOTE 筆記頁

NOTE 筆記頁

NOTE 筆記頁

NOTE 筆記頁

總經銷：朝日文化

進退貨地址：新北市中和區橋安街15巷1號7樓

TEL：(02)2249-7714 FAX：(02)2249-8715

國家圖書館出版品預行編目資料

超實用銀行英語單字／楊曜檜著. ——初版. ——臺
北市：書泉，2012.10
　　面；　　公分

　　ISBN 978-986-121-785-7（平裝）

1.英語　2.銀行業　3.詞彙

805.12　　　　　　　　　　　　　　　　101016836

3AL1
超實用銀行英語單字

作　　者	楊曜檜
發 行 人	楊榮川
總 編 輯	王翠華
文字編輯	溫小瑩
版型設計	吳佳臻
封面設計	吳佳臻

出 版 者　書泉出版社

　　地　　址：台北市大安區 106
　　　　　　　和平東路二段 339 號 4 樓
　　電　　話：(02)2705-5066（代表號）
　　傳　　真：(02)2706-6100
　　網　　址：http://www.wunan.com.tw
　　電子郵件：shuchuan@shuchuan.com.tw
　　劃撥帳號：01303853
　　戶　　名：書泉出版社

法律顧問　元貞聯合法律事務所　張澤平律師

版　　刷　2012 年 10 月　初版一刷
　　　　　2013 年 1 月　初版二刷

定　　價　300 元整　　　　　※版權所有‧請勿翻印※

總經銷:朝日文化

進退貨地址:新北市中和區橋安街15巷1號7樓

TEL:(02)2249-7714 FAX:(02)2249-8715